# NEON DRUID

## AN ANTHOLOGY OF URBAN CELTIC FANTASY

♣

EDITED BY:

I. E. KNEVERDAY

Within these pages are works of mythological fiction. Names, characters, businesses, places, events, locales, and incidents are either the products of the authors' imaginations or are being used in a fictitious manner. Any resemblance to actual persons, living or dead, or actual events is purely coincidental.



ISBN: 9781791884178

For all of the beautiful friends we've made in ugly pubs.

# WELCOME TO NEON DRUID

Please, come in from the rain and pull up a barstool. Pay no mind to Jimmy over in the corner there, he's always makin' faces at people when they walk in. There ya go. Alright, now that you're settled, allow me to formally welcome you to *Neon Druid: An Anthology of Urban Celtic Fantasy*. Rest assured that this is, indeed, a fully licensed anthology, serving only the finest in handcrafted short fiction.

On the menu tonight, we have seventeen tales set in a world where the gods, goddesses, heroes, and monsters of Celtic mythology live among us, intermingling with unsuspecting mortals and stirring up mayhem in cities and towns on both sides of the Atlantic, from Limerick and Edinburgh to Montreal and Boston.

Now, before you cross over into the Celtic Otherworld, I have a few housekeeping items that I'd be remiss not to mention:

- **Housekeeping item #1**: For the purposes of this anthology, Irish mythology, Scottish mythology, Welsh mythology, Cornish mythology, Manx mythology, and Breton mythology are all included under the "Celtic mythology" umbrella.

- **Housekeeping item #2:** All of the stories contained within these pages are either A) being published for the first time, or B) being reprinted with permission.

- **Housekeeping item #3:** Instead of creating two versions of this anthology, one for British-English readers and one for American-English readers, I opted instead to retain the native spelling preferences of each author.

Yeesh, look at me ramblin' on and on. Let's get bloody on with it already, shall we? Here, take a look at our comprehensive Story List and pick your poison. You can enjoy these stories in any order.

*Sláinte!*

**I. E. Kneverday**

Editor, *Neon Druid*

# STORY LIST

# DREAMS OF GOLD

*Madison McSweeney*

I can't see the harbour from where we are – the buildings around us are too tall and close together to provide more than a sliver of horizon – but I can smell it.

That sharp pungent scent of salt and algae intermingling with gasoline and rotted wood. If I close my eyes, the traffic on the streets outside our walls sounds like the waves sloshing against the dock; when I get in this space of mind, I can feel myself slipping back into my skin and diving back into those waters.

And then Carl barks an order and I emerge from the fog.

Carl's at the back of the bar, in the sealskin coat he stole from me, chatting with a customer underneath the TV set mounted on the wall. There's a football game flashing across the screen, and Carl doesn't avert his eyes as he points me towards one of the booths. For the first time, I notice a young woman slumped in the seat, staring at nothing.

"Has she been served?"

"I didn't see her," I reply.

Carl scoffs. "What do I pay you for?"

That jab is for the customer's benefit. Carl doesn't pay me anything at all.

I attend to the woman in the booth. She's dressed down in jeans and a grey sweatshirt, which hangs limply over an emaciated frame and protruding collarbone. Her hood is up, but her zipper's half-undone, revealing a flash of green bra.

From the club across the street, I think. The girls often come in just before or after their shifts, and order either coffee or booze, depending.

Before I can take her order, the woman puts her head on the table and starts to weep. Her hood falls slightly backward as she caresses her head in her hands, revealing a mass of red hair. I step forward tentatively, thinking I'll offer her some coffee and some comforting words. Sometimes, when these girls get roughed up, they let you call someone for them. Most of the time they don't.

I stop in my tracks when her sobs take on a sharper, shriller pitch. The keen pierces my soul, bringing back memories of the old country, of my first man's weathered grandmother, and the wild look in her eye the night she heard a wail like that.

I look back at Carl, still shooting the shit with the other customer. Say, what's that material? Sealskin? You don't see that often. If he sees the wailing woman, he doesn't show it. I suppose he's learned to tune out crying girls over the years.

In any case, he doesn't know what she is. But I know, and the knowledge frightens me.

I make a fresh pot of coffee and bring her one unprompted. "On the house," I say, placing the cup in front of her and taking the seat opposite in the booth.

She blinks her bloodshot eyes, which flick warily to my offering. "You know I don't choose," the banshee says. "I'm just a harbinger."

I nod. "I know that." The banshee wraps a trembling hand around the paper cup and takes a cautious sip. I risk a question: "Who?"

But the woman bows her head and starts to wail again. I recoil at the sound. Finally, Carl turns. "Can you keep it down over there?" In response, the woman hops up and rushes the exit, tears flowing freely, the wooden doors slamming shut behind her.

Carl rolls his eyes and resumes his business. I go back to work, periodically scanning the room and wondering who among us has been foretold to die.

♣

An hour passes with the slowness of a ticking clock with nowhere to go.

The penultimate customer leaves at halftime, gold watch glinting in the TV lights, and Carl waves me over. He cocks his head towards the man who's been sitting at the bar for the past hour, nursing a beer. From his seat on the stool, the man's short arms barely reach his glass, and his legs, dangling, don't even hit the halfway point of the chair leg.

"What's he been drinking?" Carl asks. There's a slight smirk on his face that I don't like.

"Guinness," I say, reluctantly.

Carl grins. "Of course. He's really suckin' 'em back, eh?"

I shake my head. "He's been drinking from the same glass for an hour."

Carl's brow furrows. "Odd. I always heard those things drank like fish."

"He's not a thing," I say, but Carl doesn't hear me, which is typical. He's got selective hearing that way.

"Think he'll pay in gold?" Carl asks, only half-joking

"He's more likely to slip you a fake bill," I reply. "Leprechauns don't part with their gold easily."

♣

I whittle half an hour away with a damp washcloth, trying in vain to scrub the years of residual stickiness from the dark surfaces of the tables. Behind me, the leprechaun plays solitaire and does not order another drink. Yet every time I look back, his glass is full.

I frown, finish wiping down the table, and proceed to the face of an antique mirror mounted between one of the booths. The glass is smoky with age and neglect, but its reflective quality returns with a few squirts of vinegar. Studying the mirror, I watch the image of the leprechaun take a long draught of his beer, glance at me (and I avert my eyes), look leftward at Carl (to find him distracted by the football game), and scuttle to a standing position on top of his seat. I feign distraction as the leprechaun steps onto the counter, bends over the tap and refills his glass, lithe as a cat, before settling back on the stool as if nothing had happened.

I continue cleaning the mirror. The leprechaun keeps drinking, and soon enough his glass is drained again. I watch as scrambles to the top of his chair. The second he bends over the tap, I pounce.

"Thief!" I yell, seizing him by the wrist.

Carl turns from the game, bellowing in surprise and anger. "Keep a-hold on 'him!" he shouts, and I tighten my grip on the leprechaun's arm.

Carl ambles across the room, an idiot grin on his face.

"Now, if I have my stories right..." Carl says, and glances at me pointedly; "and I usually do—you now owe me a pot o' gold."

Midnight.

The leprechaun, bound in more ways than one, sits morosely on his stool, mindlessly shuffling cards, his left foot handcuffed to the chair leg. I've given him another beer, figuring it was the least I could do.

Tomorrow, Carl says, when the sun comes out, we'll escort the leprechaun back to whatever cheap motel he calls home and make him point us towards his hiding spot. Until then, I suspect, it'll be a long night.

Carl's in a fine mood now, walking from tap to table with a spring in his step and cheering at the television whenever anyone scores a point. I'm finding it impossible to be quite as cheery: leprechauns have ways of extricating themselves from situations like this, and the banshee's grim prophecy still weighs on me.

At twelve-fifteen, a young guy in a football jersey stumbles in. I can't help but cringe. I've seen his type too many times. Goes out to a sports bar, watches the game over a half-dozen beers and a couple handfuls of nachos; his team wins, so he goes out to celebrate with his lunkhead friends; eventually, they decide to turn in for the night, and he decides he's not done. So he comes here.

It's an unwritten rule of this world: the one guy too drunk for any bartender to legally serve, always magically finds his way to the one bar willing to serve him.

The drunk staggers across the room, his steps so wide and jerky that I fear he'll trip over himself and crack his skull. Miraculously, he makes it to the bar and slurs an order, which I wait to fill until after he's fished out his credit card from his wallet. When he drinks his beer, half of it sloshes over the rim of the glass and dribbles down the front of his shirt.

"Why don't you sit down?" I say, still concerned that he's about to topple over. I point to the stool directly next to him; instead, he stumbles a few feet and lands roughly right next to the leprechaun. I wince.

The leprechaun, his humour evidently improving, spins around amicably and says, "G'd e'ening, laddie, whaddaya say ya join me fer a hand?" Smiling a rotten smile, he splays out his deck of cards.

"No funny business, leprechaun," I snap.

"Nahhh, I'll play some cards with the little man," the drunk replies. "Know any gin?"

"Why, I do," the leprechaun replies, sounding suddenly, troublingly sober. "What say we make things in'eresting?"

I glance sharply toward Carl, who's resumed his inattentiveness. I can't fathom what trickery the leprechaun's up to, but then again, it isn't my concern. In the end, this is about Carl and Carl's gold. I turn around and leave the men to their wager.

Carl was kind, once. Kind enough to lure me onto the shore, to make me feel safe enough to disrobe, to shed my skin and lie next to him in the sun. The kindness lasted only as long as it took to steal my skin and trap me. I'd been caught by men before—good, lonely men just looking for a faithful wife—and I'd been content with them for a while. Carl didn't want a wife, though; he wanted a slave.

Some believe that selkies lure men to their doom, but in my experience, it's been the other way around. The tricksters of the old world have nothing on a charming man with lies in his heart.

There's a commotion at the bar. I pivot at the sound of breaking glass.

The leprechaun's beer glass has been swept off the counter and is lying shattered on the floor. The leprechaun is sitting bolt upright on the stool, knowledge of the handcuff the only thing preventing him from making a break for it. The drunk is standing up, still tottering slightly, his finger erect and jammed in the leprechaun's face. "There ain't three ace o' spades in a deck! What're you tryin'ta pull?"

In a matter of seconds, Carl is standing over them. "Hey, what's going on here?"

"This cheating bastard cheated me!" the drunken man yells. Forgetting his chain, the leprechaun hops from the stool and moves to flee. He gazes at me imploringly, and I reach into my pocket for the key. But Carl sees me and extends his arm. "Don't you even think about it, sea-bitch!"

I'm about to dissent when the drunk screams again, a petulant child ignored by arguing parents. "I want my frigging money back!" In unison, we turn to see the gun in his hand.

The leprechaun instinctively bolts and goes flying as he exhausts the length of the chain. He lands chin-first on the hardwood, pieces of broken glass slicing the hands that break his fall.

"Can't run from me, ya little bastard!" the drunk screams, and fires.

"No!" Carl yells, and steps in front of the bullet, thinking of gold.

♣

The gunman is standing stock-still, gun lowered, hands trembling. His mouth hangs open, and his eyes are wide. A trail of urine runs down his leg and trickles into his shoe. I watch him warily, half-afraid that he's going to tie up loose ends by turning his gun on the rest of us. Instead, he yells something unintelligible and runs out the door.

Carl's body lies twitching on the floor, arms and legs shaking, blood spurting from his mouth, staining his shirt, staining his coat. I stare at that stain for a moment, before the leprechaun's voice brings me back:

"Release me, lassie! All the gold I own be yours, may you just let me out!"

I fish the key from my pocket and unhook the handcuff. "Just go," I tell him. "I've no use for your gold."

The door creaks open and clicks shut. In the distance, there's the whir of traffic, humming like the sea, and above that, sirens. A neighbour must have heard the shot. A few more seconds, and we'll be surrounded. I kneel next to Carl's body, lift his right arm, and begin to strip him of the coat.

As I take back what is mine, I find myself remembering my first man, who was kinder than Carl but still sought to trap me, and the night his grandmother heard a banshee. Seamus had been so distraught by the omen that he'd mislaid the key to his chest, and I'd found it. I fled under cover of darkness that night; I never did find out which of them had died.

I dip out the back door and escape through the alley, the coat in my arms, my footfalls echoing like gunshots on the concrete. From the corner of my eye, I can see ambulances and police trucks milling outside the bar. As I make my way down the street, I fancy that the cars are following me, and I duck behind the brick wall of a parking garage at the first flash of red and blue.

At last, the buildings disappear, and the harbour yawns in front of me. The sirens fade, and all I can hear is the water, churning and crashing against the hulls of a dozen forgotten boats.

Feeling the night wind on my bare arms for the last time, I unfurl the coat. My eyes close, and the voice of the sea swells around me. The air smells slightly of salt. I open them again and take one final look at the city, admiring the ripples of moonlight that glint against the high-rises.

Then, without regret, I slide back into my skin and dive into the water, free.

# THE FAOLADH

*Patrick Winters*

*Limerick—1897*

Their footfalls echoed up and down the streets, ringing along the cobblestones and the faces of hulking gray tenements. The glow of sporadic lamplights did little to light the night, the chilled fog in the air fighting back the feeble luminescence and keeping the city blocks in shadow. Normally, such conditions would serve them just fine, as shadow brought anonymity, and anonymity was just as useful to their trade as the well-sharpened blades they so loved to use. The trouble was, it concealed their quarry just as well, and if the boy was lost to them, he could bring a great deal of trouble upon them—be it from the clubs of some flat feet, or even the well-sharpened knives of some fellow felons, if Fate were truly against them

Quinn Kelly scanned every nook and cranny they passed, his keen eyes looking for any betrayal of hurried movement, or perhaps a shadow that didn't fit against the rest of the darkened streets. His cherished skean was clutched in his gloved hand and held low at his waist, keeping it concealed; droplets of red still slipped off its wicked tip, falling to the street-way with nary a sound.

Kelly and his cohort—a very green and very nervous lad named James Byrne—were coming upon a cross-street now; Kelly stopped in the center of the way, and he staid Byrne with a gruff hand to the chest.

"Careful, now," Kelly grumbled. "He could've gone any which

way . . ."

Byrne whipped his head about, his copper-toothed mouth all slack-jawed and his cobalt eyes all panicky.

"You think he saw what we done?"

"Aye. He ran, didn't he?"

Byrne made an effort to swallow down his anxiousness. He nearly succeeded at it; but then he went right back to wearing his guilt, and Kelly knew then and there that he'd always be too jittery for this line of business. He'd be sure to tell O'Malley as much—presuming they could remedy this unfortunate turn in their task, and that he could stand before his boss again without O'Malley putting a bullet in his gut for this mishap.

Doyle might've been more understanding in the matter if he were still the man in charge of their little enterprise. But he wasn't, as Kelly knew all too well. He'd been the one to strangle the old man, after all—something he hadn't much regretted, until right about now. Because when O'Malley had wanted to take over the gang, it seemed a wise move. He was more crafty and cunning than old Doyle, who'd been soft to start with, and who'd been growing softer each day. And O'Malley was far more ruthless, too. While Kelly had once appreciated that quality, it seemed a mite more worrisome, now that that ruthlessness might come down on his own head.

"So, what?" Doyle might've said about this particular predicament. "A blasted urchin saw you gut a worthless barrister that couldn't pay his debts to our like? The little rat is probably soiling himself in some gutter, too afraid to go to anyone about it."

But O'Malley? Certainly not. If he'd said it once, he'd said it a hundred times: "A loose end has a funny way of wrapping around your neck and seein' ya' hang." And if a loose end like this were to come back and haunt them, O'Malley would surely lynch the two of them himself, if only to make a point to the rest of their troop.

Kelly could almost feel the rope slipping about his neck in that very instant, and he didn't much care for the notion—much less the sensation.

"Quiet all that huffing!" he snarled at his panting partner. "Look about, damn it. And listen."

They stood there, easing their breaths and giving their ears to the hazy night, seeking out a tell-tale shuffling of feet or some desperately-hushed breaths that cut through the darkness. A dog barked from some ways away, its gruff *whoofs* echoing along the streets, and there was the clinking of glass and bursts of guffaws coming from Darcy's pub just up the block. And knowing Darcy's usual crowd, the racket would only increase as the late hours came calling. But aside from that, the night was eerily still.

Byrne gave an aggravated sigh. "He couldn't have just up and—"

Something skittered across stone a few feet away, and the both of them whirled about, looking to the alley at their right. Kelly lifted his skean away from the concealment of his coat in murderous anticipation. But their quarry was nowhere in sight; the noise had come from a fat and filthy rat, which was scrambling its way around the base of a lamppost. It stopped, turning its whiskered nose up at them and giving a taunting little squeak for their troubles.

Then something smacked across the street at their backs, and Kelly and Byrne spun about again.

There, standing a few yards into the opposite alley, was a short figure shrouded in shadow, its mop of dirty blonde hair just barely visible against the darkness. The rotten old shipping crate the boy had been hiding behind had come apart, its boards crashing along the cobblestones and betraying his presence.

A half-second's worth of gawking later and the boy was off again, darting down the street for all he was worth.

"After the little shite!" Kelly growled. He shoved Byrne along, and the two gave chase.

The boy was quick on his feet, but not nearly enough to outrun his pursuers. They were gaining on him, and quickly, their hurried steps clapping like hollow thunder up and down the way.

The boy ran along for another whole block, glancing back to them as he went; then, knowing they'd be upon him soon enough, he darted down a side alley and disappeared from sight.

"Keep up!" Kelly snarled at Byrne. They redirected their course, slipping into the side alley—and they were met with a fortuitous sight.

The alley—half-filled with old shipping crates and scattered refuse—was a dead end. It stretched several meters in before the buildings to either side met up at a solid brick wall, the clearance of which loomed high overhead, far out of anybody's reach. The boy was at its end, staring up at the cold, confining bricks and trembling in place. He turned about, all wide-eyed and terrified, as Kelly gave a cruel laugh.

"Nowhere left to go, lad," the thug said through a crooked grin. "If you'd just faced us like a man from the start, I'd have made what comes next quick and simple. But now that you've made us run you down . . ."

The boy started to cry silent tears, which cut salty treks along his sooty young cheeks. He pressed his back to the dead-end wall, sliding down to his haunches and covering up his head with his hands, cowering from the men as they approached.

Byrne stopped in place as he got a good, clear look at the lad. "Christ, Kelly—he's only a pup. Can't have seen more than six years, if even that!"

Kelly rolled his eyes at the show of sympathy. He raised his skean up and towards Byrne, sure that the sight of the blade would get his point across if his words shouldn't.

"Aye. A pup that could go barkin' to the law, yappin' about what he seen us do. Tellin' them all about our handsome features. And if it just so happens to be one of O'Malley's crooked clubbers he goes to? We'll have to pray that we see bars, because O'Malley would have us seein' the bottom of Abbey River, instead. Our employer is not one to have his little errands made public, boy."

Byrne glanced to the crying urchin, then back to Kelly, chewing at the inside of his lip.

"Maybe we've scared him enough to—"

"Show some guts, boy—before my dagger goes looking for them in that belly o' yours."

Byrne's face fell into meek resignation; then he inched forward again, readying to reach out for the boy and hoist him up from his spot. Kelly's smile came back as the lad sunk further to the ground, giving a quiet whine.

"Leave that boy alone!"

The voice that struck up behind them was slurred, but deep. Kelly and Byrne turned about, and both were surprised to see that there'd been another soul in the alley with them all this time.

Some vagabond had made a temporary home amidst the crates at their back, a ratty blanket for a bed and bits of garbage as his pillow. He was rising up from his grubby spot now, expending a fair deal of effort to do so, it seemed, and looking on them with something like sluggish loathing. The man looked to be middle-aged, his dirtied face sagging with wrinkles and years, wherever his bushy beard didn't cover up. His long dark hair hung about his head in matted clumps. It was hard to gauge his bulk and frame; the old furs and grimy scraps of cloth that made up his clothes hung loosely over him. His big hands were covered by frayed gloves, the fingers of which looked to have been torn and shredded off. His brown boots were in as rough a state, his toes practically peeking out of the worn leather as he shambled forward, stepping over towards Kelly and Byrne.

"Are you drunk, friend?" Kelly laughed. "Or just a fool? Probably never would'a seen you there, if you'd kept your trap shut. Now, we're gonna' have to gut you, too."

The man's eyes rolled up into the back of his head, and he nearly fell on his face as he fought to keep his balance. It seemed he might've been snuggling up with a bottle, after all.

"Get away . . . from the boy," he grumbled. "Go! Or . . . else . . ."

"Ah—threats, now!" Kelly sauntered up to the vagabond, bobbing his dagger about in his hand. Byrne stood in place, looking more and more uncertain about this whole evening and the troubles it'd brought.

"What? Comin' over to breathe on us? Savin' the lad with your fumes?"

Kelly gave another laugh as the homeless man kept stumbling towards him, groaning with the effort. But the criminal's grin fell away when the man reached a trembling hand out at him, fingers fanning as though to grab or scratch at him.

"All right—enough's enough," Kelly sneered. "Time to give you a good home. Up there, with the good Lord."

And with that, Kelly darted forward, evading the vagabond's grasp and sending his knife up into the man's gut. The man gave a pained holler and crumpled into himself, and Kelly took the chance to send his knife right back into him, up around the kidneys, and every time the man recoiled, he snuck in another jab or a quick cut. When the man finally fell to the ground, he curled up into a fetal position, moaning in anguish.

Kelly gloated over him as he steadily went still.

"It's a shame, really—all the trash in our streets." Kelly gave a shrug and turned back around, his attention returning to the cowering boy. "Now, where were we?"

The thug had taken only a couple steps forward before he noticed Byrne, who was still looking over towards the dead vagrant.

"What are you gawkin' about?" Kelly snapped.

Byrne blinked, looking rather amazed. "He's *still movin'*."

Kelly looked over his shoulder, and he was perplexed to see that Byrne was right; the dead man apparently wasn't dead enough, after all. His legs were twitching, and his sides were rising and falling, but not quite like they would with the lull of breathing. It seemed more like something was . . . shifting beneath his clothes . . . moving all about . . .

Kelly slunk back towards the vagabond, on his guard for any trick at hand. As he drew closer, he leaned down, knife held before him, ready to send it into the homeless man's side once more.

And that's when he heard the rising of a deep, grumbling growl.

In the blink of an eye, the vagabond was leaping up from the ground, slashing out at Kelly with a canine's snarl. The hand that came swiping across Kelly's upper chest had changed from any ordinary hand to that of a creature's claw—the skin gone all gray and rough and covered with hair, the fingers extended by another good inch and having sharpened nails that cut like dagger tips. Those very nails tore away at Kelly's vest and shirt, finding the meat and bone beneath and pulling it all away in a flash of agony.

Kelly fought to scream as he fell back along the ground, but managed only some flustered gurgles as blood bubbled out of him, sleeking along his torso. He held a hand up to his grievous wound, scooting himself away from the vagabond as the latter rose up to his feet, looming taller and steadier than before. Kelly was horrified to see that it wasn't the vagabond's hazy eyes that looked down at him, but those of some mythic beast of lore: all black and piercing, and set into the great face of some wolf-like terror. The animal-man's black nose sniffed at him from the end of a long muzzle, and it bared its impossible teeth at him as it kept up its growling, saliva dribbling out from its mighty jaws.

It stepped towards him with slow and menacing paces, as a wolf would when stalking its prey.

"Jesus!"

The wolf-man's head snapped to the side, looking over to Byrne as he called out to God for salvation. The young thug was scrambling backwards, fumbling for the knife stowed away in his own coat pockets. He gave a surprised holler as he smacked into the dead-end wall, knocking the cowering boy aside in his futile effort to flee. The boy cried out from the sudden blow and fell to the ground; and in that instant, the wolf-man leapt at Byrne, letting loose a snapping growl that was filled with an unholy fury.

Byrne screamed as the creature fell upon him, raking its claws across his stomach and letting loose a waterfall of red. Then it grabbed hold of his shoulders and lifted him over its head with staggering might; it threw him right into the opposing wall of the alley, and Byrne crumpled to the ground in a broken pile. But the creature, like a bloodhound with the scent of its hunt, did not let up. It dove onto Byrne, its great back to Kelly, and it proceeded to rip and tear away at the still-screaming criminal—until his screams ceased altogether.

Kelly, not intent to suffer the same fate as his young partner, set his belly to the ground and tried to crawl away, keeping one hand to his ruined chest and hauling himself along with his other arm. The street was cold beneath him, and he could already feel that deathly chill spreading throughout the rest of his trembling frame.

Lost to his fear, he swore to Heaven above that he would renounce his devious ways and do whatever it took to make amends in the eyes of God, if only he could be spared from this terrible beast.

But if his prayers reached Heaven, they fell on deaf ears—for no sooner had Byrne's cries ceased than Kelly heard a taunting growl from over his shoulder. He turned around, knowing full well what awaited him; but he screamed all the same as the wolf-man brought its claws down upon him…

♣

When Declan came back to himself, he was not surprised to see that he was kneeling by a dead man—the very one who had, in fact, tried to kill him.

It was not the first time the Wolf within had asserted its violent desires upon violent men, and he imagined it would not be the last, as violent men seemed to pop up everywhere, no matter which part of the land he tried to lose himself in. And while the results of the transformation had been horrible and messy, as always, at least there was this: the child these men had sought to harm had been protected. And on that, he and the Wolf could both be satisfied. As to why the Wolf should care for the life of any human child, Declan hadn't the slightest notion; but it had been adamant in its call to action, and when the men refused to heed his attempted warning, the Wolf had refused to heel within his bones any longer.

Groaning, Declan rose up to his feet, his muscles strained from the

Wolf's exertions and his raggedy clothes covered in blood. He took in the sight of the dead man at his feet with a sad and weary sigh, and he looked upon the body of the other, younger hooligan in much the same way.

A quiet sniffling caught Declan's attention. It was the boy, still laying along the ground where he'd fallen, hiding his face against his arms and crying into them.

Feeling a swell of pity, Declan stepped over towards the lad. He moved slowly, his body still tingling and aching from the tremendous change he'd undergone; even after all these years, he still hadn't grown accustomed to the transformation—and he believed that he never would. He pulled off his long and outermost coat as he went; it had taken the brunt of the dead men's blood, and he let it fall to the ground, its usefulness spent and its state far too horrible for the boy to see. And God knew, the lad had already seen too damned much this night.

Declan pulled off his ruined gloves, mopping up the blood that was still on his fingertips, and then tossed them aside. He crouched down beside the boy, setting a cautious and gentle hand to the youth's shoulder.

"It's over, lad," he told him, trying for as soothing and kind a tone as he could muster. "No harm is gonna' come to you now. I promise you that."

The boy rubbed at his face before peeking up to Declan, and when Declan opened up his arms to him, the youngster slowly sat up. He wrapped his arms around Declan's neck, and the *faoladh* hauled him up, holding the boy close and repeating his promise to keep him from harm. Then Declan turned and headed out of the alley, making sure that the boy shut his eyes and looked away from the dead men as they passed them by.

"We'll get you somewhere safe," he told the boy as they walked along the foggy city streets.

And from somewhere within the depths of Declan's bones, the Wolf gave a contented sigh.

# THE FLAT ABOVE THE WYND

*Alexandra Brandt*

Originally Published in *The Faerie Summer*, 2017

Sky glared at the (entirely too long) spiral of chipped red stairs and cursed Ram once more.

Not aloud, mind you, and not with any real intent. Being only half Wyndling meant she wasn't terribly strong in magic, but she'd rather not risk her theoretical cursing becoming a *real* fairy curse through sheer carelessness. Especially not when her beloved former mentor was enjoying a well-deserved retirement in the Wynd.

She hoped.

But right now, she desperately wished him here by Lady Stairs. Because she wanted his counsel, especially now as she was trying to pick up where he left off. Because she missed Ramsay "Old White" Whitebridge more than her own long-absent father.

And, most importantly, because she *really* wanted to give Ram a piece of her mind.

He could have had a flat anywhere in Edinburgh's Old Town, as long as there was an active human close or wynd nearby. By the end of his 300-year tenure as Protector of all the Sideways along the Royal Mile, he had a *very* comfortable living from his long-term investments.

Sky knew this, because it was all hers now.

So, when he could have had any flat he chose, why had he chosen Lady Stairs Close?

Her ire wasn't about the long flight of stairs, not really. Any location along the Royal Mile would have that problem, since there would always be shops below. (Although he *could* have chosen something other than the very, very top.)

It was just that this spot was so…*central.*

So full of people. All the time.

People always trying to climb *these* bloody stairs. Because someone had helpfully labeled them and now the damn tourists thought they were part of the Lady Stairs Close experience. Lovely green James Court, even more picturesque honey-and-smoke-colored Makar's Court, the Writers' Museum…and the red stairs that *clearly* must be the famed Lady Stairs the close was named for.

(They were not.)

Sky liked people. She liked the noise and color and bustle of Old Town, from the nigh-constant drone of the bagpipes to the crack of the street performer's whips to the sidewalks cluttered with displays of tartans and kilts from the dozen wool-and-cashmere shops that populated her block alone. Unlike many of her former (human) coworkers from the banking job, she even liked these late-summer crowds of tourists.

But she didn't like them climbing the stairs to her flat. Every day. All day.

*So why here, Ram?* Sky would never in a million years try to use Lady Stairs to cross over into the Wynd—it was far too popular, although its popularity certainly gave it more power than some of the other Sideways. And now she would have to be extra careful about her appearance *in her own home,* with the risk of random folk coming up the stairs…and possibly seeing a silhouette that didn't look…human.

Not to mention the inconvenience right at this very moment, waiting for the most recent tourist—English, she thought—to realize he was blocking the way to her flat. Walloper. No clue he was keeping her from her job, of course.

Which was *not* to be standing at the foot of the stairs and wishing she was elsewhere.

Her job was to go upstairs, look into the Eye, read a few more pages of the stacks and stacks of notes Ram left her…and then don her amulets and be ready to start her patrol by late afternoon.

Before the dusk and the twilight.

When doors might open.

When anything could happen.

She tried to block out the chatter and steps on the stairs—here came another group, kids this time, just lovely, thanks—and concentrate on what she was reading.

Wynd Law was infinitely more twisty and tricky than she'd ever imagined. And she had learned quite a lot of it, growing up with one foot in Edinburgh and one in the Wynd; with her status as a half-Wyndling, she'd known to be careful. But as Protector—albeit an unofficial one—her responsibilities now tripled. And, if she wanted to keep doing Ram's work without fear of interference from the Wynd, the laws that bound her tripled too.

Laws she had already broken, less than a month ago.

She hadn't known better. She hadn't even known she would be assuming Ram's mantle at the time. So she had let two teenagers, two Lost Children, go back home with their memories intact…and now she had no idea how that would affect her future.

If other Wyndlings ever found out, that is.

A faint glow pulsed from the Far-Seeing Eye, and Sky welcomed the chance to stop rubbing her temples and look at her first location for patrol.

The documents Ram had left her about the Eye vaguely said it was 'tuned to receive echoes of possible futures,' which sounded like it *ought* to mean something. What it meant in practical terms was the Eye sent her an image of somewhere in Old Town…and most often, nothing would happen when she got there.

On the days something *did* happen, however…

Luckily there had been no repeats of that first, fateful incident.

Yet.

She picked up the circle of normally-milky glass and peered into it. The misty depths had cleared, revealing…the foot of her own stairs?

She frowned and shook it. Had her own internal complaints affected it, somehow?

Impossible. There were too many safeguards on this, the most necessary of her Protector's tools. The Eye was even keyed to this very flat, so it would vanish and return here should it ever be forcefully removed from Sky's possession. She could only imagine the kind of power that would go into a spell like that. Her own meagre abilities couldn't compare.

The disc pulsed with pale light again, revealing the same image. No question about it, they were the red-painted steps she had glared at less than an hour ago.

The pulses of light came faster, somehow insistent. The Eye had never done that before.

Fine and well and good. Grimacing, Sky stood and drew on her faded green summer-weight anorak, stuffing the disc of glass into a hidden inner pocket and tucking Ram's jumble of amulets down her shirt. She checked her glamour in the mirror—yes, still the ordinary brown skin and brown eyes of a mid-thirty-ish East Indian woman; no odd blue eyes or furred, plume-like tail to be seen—and grumbled to herself as she exited the flat and headed for the stairs.

Because of the twisty nature of the stairwell, Sky almost ran into the girl standing at the base, frowning down at a slip of paper in her hand. A slight, dark-haired teenager with a pretty face, possibly Japanese heritage. Ripped jeans and a black t-shirt with some rock band or another, heavy satchel over one shoulder.

Sky knew her instantly.

The girl looked up and her eyes widened. "You!"

Sky tried to school her shock into something calmer. She had never thought she'd see this child again.

Not after what they'd been through, merely three weeks before.

"What are you doing here?" Sky asked, her mind racing. At the back of her head, a thought began to flash, a reminder of the Wynd law she had just read. The rules she had broken with this very human girl. And now, a sudden, serendipitous opportunity to fix things.

With Wynd magic, serendipity should *always* be highly suspect.

So.

She needed more information.

The girl was still frozen, surprise written all over her face. "I—" She shook her head, as if trying to clear it. "I—hang on. What are *you* doing here?" More likely American tourist than Canadian, Sky thought, revising her first impression from last month.

Sky ignored the girl's clumsy deflection. "I thought you were going home. You said you left the next day." She remembered the conversation very clearly. The girl and her (Sky assumed) blond boyfriend had been shaken from the near-kidnapping they had just experienced—but of the two of them, the girl had seemed the more quick-witted at the time.

"Kevin left. I stayed." The girl chewed her lip, looking down at her hands, which clenched and unclenched. Sky wondered if the short response hid still-fresh pain over a breakup.

"Why?" Sky asked, more gently. "Why would you stay? You know it's not safe."

"Oh no, I was careful! I didn't come back to the Royal Mile," the girl protested. "I mean—" she turned red as Sky arched an eyebrow and looked around pointedly. "Not until now. I had to get answers. I had to know what happened. And I couldn't find you again, and..." she trailed off, and looked at her hands again.

Sky kept her bearing, but inside her emotions churned. What a right bourach this was, as Ram would say. A mess *she* had made because she hadn't known what she was doing in the slightest.

She'd need to do better, this time.

Much better.

The girl looked up, chewing her lip once more. She glanced around at the people milling about Makar's Court beyond the stairwell, then back at Sky. "I guess...can we talk somewhere more private?" she asked. She peered upstairs, past Sky's shoulder.

Privacy was a very good idea, but the girl was *not* getting invited to Sky's flat.

Unless you just erased her memories afterward, a small part of her mind whispered. Sky pushed the thought aside, not liking the queasy feeling it produced.

She didn't *want* this kind of responsibility.

"Follow me," Sky said, moving past the girl and into the late afternoon sunlight. Her patrol would normally begin soon. But the Eye had clearly wanted her here, and for good reason.

Still, best to be sure. She surreptitiously tugged the disc from her pocket, noting that it had turned milky again. Good enough.

"By the way," Sky said, pausing before they entered the sidewalks, "What's your name? You can call me Sky."

The girl turned red again. "Oh shit—I mean, uh. I hadn't even thought of that." She stuck out a hand. "I'm Morgan."

Sky took Morgan's hand and smiled encouragingly. "I didn't think of it myself. We *were* a bit busy. Now follow me; I've got just the spot for a chat—if you don't mind about seven minutes of walking."

Trunk's Close was both old and quiet, making it one of the better Sideways. But when it wasn't being used for that purpose, it was also the way into a little public garden: one of her favorite places in the world, and seldom populated by tourists.

Today was no exception. Sky would never grow tired of the way the clamor of the streets seemed to vanish when one stepped into the closes and courts that led off from the spine that was The Royal Mile. No magic needed; the old stones and structures of the city itself did the work.

But she felt power humming through her bones all the same. The quiet, slow power that lay in Edinburgh, grown from the weight of history, the humans who lived and died and believed in things unseen, back and back to the medieval roots of the city. The power that Wyndlings like Sky and Ram could draw on, when they stepped into the Wynd and back again.

And for Sky, the power was love. Love for this place, love for the humans in it.

And *that* was what had called her to take on Ram's mantle, despite her fears.

It was good to remember that.

She stepped into the garden, Morgan walking quietly behind her. The sound of the streets faded into the relative hush of the green space, the rustle of the great oak tree that graced most of the garden.

Morgan peered around her with wide eyes. "I didn't even know this was here," she said, her voice soft. Sky wondered if she could feel it too. The weight, the stillness. *Could* humans feel the old power of Edinburgh, and simply not have a name for it?

Sky had no one to ask but Morgan…and now was not the time.

"Now," she said, gesturing to the bench, "Let's start. How did you find me?"

Morgan frowned. "Wait, I thought I got to ask *you* questions."

Teenagers.

"Let's make it a two-way conversation," Sky said, managing to suppress an eye-roll. "I need to know what brought you to Lady Stairs. Especially when you knew you should be avoiding Old Town."

"It was the group I found online. You know, the support group."

The *what?*

"I'm sorry, what support group?"

"The group for other people like me. People who," the girl gulped, and lowered her voice to a whisper. "Uh. Who've *crossed over into the fairy realm.*" She muttered something else under her breath that Sky couldn't quite catch.

But Sky's mind was reeling already.

Shit.

Bollocks.

And other words of which Sky's dear mother would strongly disapprove.

What was Sky supposed to do? No one had warned her about this. She'd no idea such a thing existed.

*You know what you have to do,* that voice in the back of her head whispered. Damage control.

*You have to find the whole group and erase all of those dangerous memories.*

Morgan peered at her face, frowning. "Um, Sky? Are you all right?"

She had not thought to school her expression into something properly neutral.

And there was no way to bluff her way out of this, especially with this burning need to know *exactly* what the teenager was talking about. Sky was going to have to use at least partial honesty, now. "I actually was unaware of the existence of a support group," she said, and her concerned frown did not need to be faked. "If they had my address, they should have contacted me." She started to build an argument for why Morgan should get the group together and take her to them immediately, but was arrested by the girl's next words.

"Oh, so that *was* your address? It was supposed to be this old white-haired guy. That's what the others said."

For the second—no, third—time today, Sky felt like she'd been hit with a sledgehammer.

*Ram* had known about this?

Morgan was still talking. "…but when I saw you, it kind of went out my head because I knew you and, you know, you were the one I wanted to talk to all along anyway. Do you know an old white-haired guy?"

*Dammit, Ram. I need you back here.*

More than ever.

"I do," Sky said, quickly getting her thoughts untangled. "He protected Old Town before me. He did what I do now."

Morgan's voice was hushed. "You—you save people who were…kidnapped by fairies. So he did that too. That makes sense."

Sky nodded. Watching over Old Town was her true purpose. And she needed to protect it at all costs; she couldn't forget that.

"Is he…dead?" the girl asked.

"Just retired," Sky assured her. Retired and well beyond her grasp. Deep in the Wynd now, bound by the very laws he had enforced, never to return to the human city again. She might see him again in a year or so, if she was lucky. It stung still.

Especially now that she suspected it had been a forced retirement. For a purpose she hadn't yet uncovered.

And now there was this.

A new mystery on her hands.

"I guess I should tell them," Morgan said slowly. "They have old information." She brightened, no doubt pleased to be of some use.

Time to seize the opportunity while she could. "I could speak to them too," Sky said. "If Ram—that's the old man—was a friend of theirs, then I should be a part of this."

The list of questions was growing by the second, but at least she had her next move sorted.

♣

The prospect of introducing the support group to Sky had apparently driven the rest of the girl's questions out of her head, which was extremely convenient. They found a cafe with free wi-fi so Morgan could get out her laptop and contact the other members.

The drinks had just arrived—tea for Sky, of course, and coffee for the American—when she felt a warm pulse in her inner coat pocket, and grimaced. She had nearly forgotten the rest of her job.

The Eye showed her an area near St. Giles' Cathedral. "I have to go keep watch again," she told Morgan, reluctantly. "Do you have a phone you can use here?"

The American shook her head. "Just my brother's, and he's still working at the University, I think. He's usually there until seven."

Sky filed that information away for later. "Why don't you arrange a meeting with your group and then contact me later, when you can borrow his phone," she said.

She needed time to think, anyway.

She had far, far too much to try to understand.

As dusk started to fall—fairly late, of course, because it was a summer evening—Sky paced near St. Giles' Cathedral, thinking furiously.

Ram had clearly been involved with this so-called "support group," and had not said a word to her about it. He clearly hadn't followed Wynd law, either. Why?

Much as she loved the sly old goat, Old White was as tricky as any other Wyndling out there. He most likely had some canny plan she couldn't possibly understand with her slightly-too-human brain.

Damn him. This put her in a terrible bind.

Her phone rang—at the same moment that the Eye pulsed against her chest.

She juggled the two inexpertly, nearly attempting to put the glass disc to her ear. Finally she managed to sort them out and answer the unfamiliar number before the ringing stopped. "It's me," said Morgan's breathless voice on the other end. "This is really weird."

"What's weird?" Sky said, squinting at the Eye's image. It still showed the very area where she stood. She felt no change to the magic all around her. No increases of power at any of the closes or wynds nearby.

How very concerning, especially taken with its behavior earlier today.

"Ravi said I shouldn't trust you, that you were lying. I told him that was bullshit," she said indignantly, but Sky heard it with half an ear, trying to walk a little further down, get a better view of the street side with the higher number of closes. "He said that the old guy, Ramsay something-or-other, hadn't retired because he just spoke to him, like, three days ago!"

Sky stopped short, right there on the crowded walk. Several passersby cursed and stumbled around her.

Impossible.

Under Wynd law, his retirement had been final. He had given over his responsibilities, his flat, his wealth and all of his magical items, over to her.

Hadn't he?

What *was* the old man's game?

"Sky? Are you still there?"

"Yes, yes—I just don't know why he'd be here," Sky said. "I was with him when he signed everything over to me." She didn't know why she was telling the child this. Just thinking out loud. Nothing made sense.

"Ravi said the old man had finally come around," Morgan said. "That—that after years of trying to convince him, he was finally letting the..." her voice faded out, then came back. "First wave? I think? Letting us—them, I mean—cross back over again." Her voice dropped to a nearly inaudible whisper with the last words.

The phone slipped out of Sky's nerveless fingers and clattered to the ground.

This was insanity.

No humans ever crossed back over a second time. Every Wyndling knew it was too dangerous, for the Wynd and for the humans themselves.

It had never occurred to her that a human would want to. Especially the Lost Children, the ones taken against their will.

But...she realized now, suddenly: Morgan had said that very thing, in the garden.

Sky had barely heard it, barely noticed while her brain had been churning with everything else. "*Who've crossed over into the fairy realm...and want to go back.*"

Oh, this was much, much worse than she had thought.

Sky picked up the phone with trembling fingers. The screen was cracked, but it still looked functional. The call was still going. "Sky? Sky? What happened?"

The Eye flared again.

"Did he say *where* they were going?" If it was happening right now, or soon, maybe that was what the Eye was trying to tell her.

"No, but I followed them. I think we're going to one of the...closes by the cathedral?"

Sky couldn't draw breath to speak. Her gaze was pulled up the street, to Byre's Close, where a stooped old man in a kilt, with wild, white hair, was unlocking the private gate and gesturing to a young East Indian man standing behind him, carrying some kind of case.

And—yes. Skye's eyes were Wyndling-sharp. There was the slim figure in the black t-shirt, trailing them half a block back.

"Morgan, I need you to go back, out of Old Town, and stay with your brother," she choked out, already dodging pedestrians and wayward vehicles on her way across the street. "I've got to talk to Ram before—" before what? He did something foolish, dangerous, possibly evil?

"But I could—"

She tried to stay calm. "This is between me and Ram, understand? Let me handle it. I'll call this number back later. All right?"

"Okay, but—" Morgan said, and Sky threw her phone into her pocket without another word.

The magic flared inside Byre's Close. Sky reached the locked gate and looked around quickly. No sign of Morgan, but she hadn't been close enough to get pulled through. Sky couldn't waste any more minutes looking around for the girl.

She used a bit of not-very-finessed power to get the gate unlocked again. It cost her precious moments, and the magic from the Sideway was already fading again by the time she got inside.

She hadn't even thrown on her "forget me," so curious heads were turning to watch her rush. She stumbled in a little further, pulling the glamour over herself. Out of sight, out of mind.

Then she stilled herself long enough to feel the power in the bones of the city. Joy and pain and memory, creativity and belief and the weight of history. This was what drew Wyndlings to the old, old closes and wynds and courts; this was what kept the Sideways open, year after year. A connection no one could explain.

She closed her eyes and let the magic pull her across into the Wynd.

Stepping into the Spine, the Wyndside equivalent to the Royal Mile, was always a disorienting experience. Colors were too bright, even in the pale green light of fairy dusk, and seemed to carry tangible weight, even taste. The buildings echoed those on the human side, but only just. They were the wrong sizes or materials, or sometimes simply impossible by the laws of physics.

Pipes wailed on this street-side, too, but their sound was wilder even than human bagpipes. Sweet and wild and eerie, and their player was a silvery creature with a few too many arms and gossamer cobweb wings. Whirring filled the air and Sky ducked a flight of tiny winged beings, what the humans would likely call pixies.

The air tasted like honey and felt like the brush of silk against her skin.

As she always did, Sky recalled vividly the first time she had crossed over. As a clueless teenager herself, only just discovering her incomprehensible paternal heritage.

In all the years following, these first few seconds Wyndside never lost their potency. Like a strong whiskey…for *all* the senses.

Sky forced herself to reorient, to focus. She had to find Ram, but he was nowhere to be seen. He'd be Old White here, in his true form, a towering half-man with goat-gargoyle feet and horns curling in his wild white mane of hair.

She didn't see any of that.

"Oh, *wow.*"

Oh, no. Skye whirled around, her stomach dropping.

Of course. Morgan. She must have followed Sky in while her eyes were closed. How could she have been so stupid? Both of them. *Stupid.*

Morgan's eyes were huge as she spun in a slow circle. "I had forgotten," she whispered. "I had forgotten how *magical* it was. Everything's so…God. I don't even know. So real. And unreal. At the same time. Like a drug."

"You can't be here!" Sky shouted. Morgan flinched and jerked back toward her.

"You don't—"

"It's dangerous, Morgan," Sky said, interrupting whatever stupid teenager thing was about to come out of the girl's mouth. "You shouldn't even need me to tell you that."

Morgan stared at her. "You're so beautiful. I forgot that too."

Sky's own changes were much more subtle than a full Wyndling. Her true self was Summer Sky Blue: golden-furred ears and silken tail added to her usual human appearance, eyes changed to a color so blue as to be unnatural.

It was normally a relief to drop her glamour here, but not today.

"We don't have time for this," she snapped. She grabbed Morgan's hand. Whatever else happened here, she couldn't risk letting the child out of her sight.

She drew her breath to shout for Ram, but something stopped her. Raised voices, up the street, toward the crystal-hued Wynd equivalent of Edinburgh Castle.

"Where is Ram Whitebridge?" a very human male voice shouted. "What kind of trick is this?"

Sky started to run toward the voice, dragging Morgan with her. She didn't dare tell the human girl to stay here in the Spine. It would be just as dangerous as not, and then Sky wouldn't be around if something happened.

There were no good solutions to this.

"I think someone is snatching your friends," she said grimly to the girl, whose eyes were still huge, her head craning from side to side as they ran. "Using trickery."

As opposed to the sheer balls that Fae Lord Alabaster had used last month, simply opening a Sideway and pulling Morgan and her boyfriend through as they ducked inside Bailie Fyfe's Close to escape a downpour.

Did that mean this was more of the same, but the criminal element had simply gotten sneakier when they realized Skye would oppose them?

Either way, it didn't bode well.

The shouts cut off abruptly, but Sky could follow where they had been. She rounded down a side street, Morgan in tow.

The alley led to a Wyndside court. Here, that meant a seat of power.

Bad. Very, very bad.

The young man who had been with not-Ram was there, gripping his case and gesturing wildly. His face was shouting, but no sound emerged. The other figure with him was like no one Sky had ever seen.

Like many of the lords of the Wynd, the figure wore flowing robes instead of the modern human fashions adopted by many other denizens of the Wynd. These robes were red. Vivid red, deep red, blood and carmine all together. The being inside them was snow-white, paler even than Alabaster had been. On its strangely-elongated head was an intricate tangle of white branches. Its hair? Or merely a headdress?

The Wyndling looked up as Sky approached. She filled her lungs to shout at it, to use the trick she had used before. Draw attention, get Wynd law to come into the picture. Pretend she had all the authority of the Protector behind her.

She never had the chance.

"Be still," the white being hissed.

Its eyes flared bright gold and blue and red, a kaleidoscope of colors. They trapped her, and the shout died in her throat.

Beside her, Morgan went still as well.

The Wyndling cocked its head at the three of them. "This will be fun," it said softly, and made a gesture with its hand.

The world flared white.

♣

She was trapped in a crystal cage. Shifting colors everywhere gave the impression of a thousand prisms, although when she touched the wall of her cell it was porous to the touch, like lava rock. There were no seams, no windows, nothing but the changing light. And her two dazed companions, clutching each other and staring wildly around them.

Like everything Wyndside, it was beautiful, shifty, and frustrating.

She resisted the urge to scream her frustration. How could she have ever thought she was strong enough, clever enough to take on Old White's mantle with only a quarter of his Wyndling power, if that?

Her amulets and the Eye were gone, of course.

The only power she possessed without them was her affinity for the magic of the Sideways, her love for Edinburgh, and the power that rested within.

She had none of that here.

She looked over at the two humans and tried to keep a calm face, for them. It was all she could do.

"I'm sorry," Morgan whispered. "I didn't know…I thought you were just going to talk to your friend, so I came to…to get Ravi."

*You came because you wanted to cross over again,* Sky thought. But rebukes would do no good here. This situation was consequence enough.

The other one, the young man, broke out of his reverie. "I—" he stumbled around, searching for words. "I'm Ravi. You must be Sky."

"I am."

"You knew the real Ram?"

"He was my mentor. He's in retirement now. I didn't lie about that, you know." She kept her voice gentle when it really wanted to go sharp.

To distract herself from her annoyance, she looked at Ravi's case. Curiously, it and Morgan's satchel were still with them, whereas all of Sky's items had been stripped of her. They even took her favorite anorak. Bastards.

Her amulets were likely lost forever, but Sky fervently hoped that the Far-Seeing Eye's safeguard spell would work. No telling what the Wyndling Lord might attempt to do with an artifact like that.

No telling how Sky could ever hope to do her job without it.

She couldn't think about that, so she pointed to the case. "What's in that?"

Ravi ducked his head. "My flute," he said. "Ram—I mean, that…*person*…told me to bring it with me. I thought he was *Ram*, so I did."

Curious, but not useful.

"Anything of use in your satchel, Morgan?" She asked. Of course there wouldn't be, not for their situation, but it gave them something to do.

"Ah—no, not really," the girl said sheepishly. "Just my art supplies, mostly."

Art supplies?

Sky realized how little she knew about this human girl she'd attached to herself. "So you're an artist…" she said, and looked back at Ravi. "And a musician."

"The others are all like that too," Morgan said, eagerly. "I figured that out right away. Everyone in the support group. We paint and sing and compose music, and I think Emma sculpts. Peter writes poetry. Isn't that weird?"

It was.

"Ram helped us," Ravi said. "The real Ram, I mean. Some of us had met him, from before. When we crossed over. For some of us he came and got us."

"Like what you did for Kevin and me," Morgan put in.

"After we started talking to each other, making this group, he helped us…" Ravi searched for words. "Channel our energies, I think he said. To remember the fairyland…I mean, the Wynd, when we made our art and music and writing. To put it all in there. And it did help," he said, misinterpreting Sky's astonished expression, "But I think we…we all wanted to go back. Some part of each of us did, even though it had been beyond scary for most of us."

Morgan nodded, looking ashamed. "I'm sorry. But it's true. I wasn't kidding when I said it was like a drug. It gets into your blood. It's like this wild…dream, or image, in the back of your mind. All the time."

"Or a song," Ravi said.

Sky found herself speechless. She never knew.

And what *had* Ram been up to? If the very memory of the Wynd was like a drug, why had he not spared them of it by taking it away?

"Ram said," Ravi added, breaking into her confused thoughts, "that what we did helped him. And the Wynd. No, that's not quite right. It helped make the doorways stronger, he said. For one day when there would be no danger in traveling them again." His voice dipped into Ram's cadence for a moment.

What did that—what did *any* of this—mean? None of the answers made any more sense than the questions.

She needed to find Ram and ask him everything.

Which meant she—and the humans—needed to get out of here.

Strengthening the Sideways. Why? And *how?*

Regardless, it did them no good now. She would give an entire leg to be near a Wyndside Close right now. A Sideway. That was where her power was. That was where she could be of use.

Then it dropped in on her. One little, silly idea.

Could they *make* a Sideway?

Would it hurt to try?

"Morgan," she said. "Get out your art supplies. Let's see if you've got enough to paint on the wall."

The shifting lights were annoying, but the wall *should* hold paint. Or charcoal. Hopefully they would be able to see it.

"Ravi. Do you know any classic jigs or reels? And how about 'Scotland the Brave?'"

Ravi nodded. "I like that kind of music," he said. "It's why I came to school here in the first place." The look on his face remained mystified.

"We're going to try to make our own Sideway," Sky told them.

Morgan looked up from sorting her pastels and charcoal sticks. "Because our art strengthens the doors," she said. Her eyes were huge. "Do you think it will work?"

"No idea," Sky said honestly. "But it's better than waiting for whatever the bloody snow creature wants from us."

"Bloody snowman," Morgan snickered, and started to smear her charcoal sticks over one wall, creating an outline. Even as rough strokes indicating an archway, the lines took on a beautiful quality under the lights. The colors filled in the 'stones' like stained glass.

Through the archway, Morgan started to sketch buildings. "Try a wool merchant," Sky said. She could picture it in her head, the one near where the piper most often played. Not far from her new flat at

Lady Stairs. She started describing it to Morgan, who filled in the colors and shapes like a rough impressionist painting.

"Your turn, Ravi," Sky said. She didn't know if music would draw the Wyndlings, but it was all they had. "Start playing 'Scotland the Brave.'" It was a very tired tune, partly because it was one of the songs the bagpipes always played outside her flat. It also sounded quite odd on the flute, but she did her best to work past that, imagining the piper in her head, playing alongside. She closed her eyes and imagined the wool merchant storefront, the piles of colorful tartans. The bustle of the street and the old, musty stones of the close as she looked out into it.

"Oh my god," Morgan whispered.

Sky didn't open her eyes. But she could *feel* it.

The love. The magic. The connection that drew Wynd and Old Town together.

Morgan took her hand and started walking forward. Sky reached out, imagining stone beneath her fingers. She could hear the pipes now.

Power flared. She heard shouts coming from somewhere. Behind her. She ignored them, drawing on the power of her imagined close…

And pulled them through.

"We did it," Morgan said in awe. Sky opened her eyes. To her right, past Morgan's wide-eyed stare, she could see Lady Stair's close, full of humans and color and noise. To her left stood Ravi, mouth agape.

They'd done it.

Sky smiled, and then frowned.

The angle and tone of the light told her it was mid-morning. Which morning? How long had they been gone? She glanced around quickly as reality crashed back in. Had any humans seen the three of them appear out of nothing?

No one seemed to be staring in shock. Perhaps their luck continued to hold. Perhaps—

"Oh, *shit,*" Morgan said, glancing down at her now-dead phone. "Nate is going to *kill* me."

Not good. And worse, the hair on the back of Sky's neck began to prickle. There was a good chance that someone—or some*thing*—would be coming through a nearby close at any moment. Not Lady Stair's; that would be madness, surely.

All the same…

She reached for the hands of Morgan and Ravi on either side of her. She would *not* relinquish them. They needed safety. They needed time to regroup.

Which meant she was going to have to let the humans into her flat, after all.

The sensible Wyndling in the back of Sky's mind gave a tiny sigh of defeat. Fine and well and good.

"Come with me," Sky said grimly.

♣

To her vast relief, the Eye's safeguards *had* held.

For there it was, back in her flat, the innocuous glass disc resting on the cheap wood of her table as if she had merely left it there from her preparations of the previous afternoon. (Had it been the previous afternoon?)

The Eye's surface was still. Yet another relief. It told her that all was well, for now.

Without its power, she didn't know what she would have done.

If she could have done anything at all.

Behind her, Morgan swore again. "It's not the battery. Sky, what should I—"

"Here." Sky shook her head clear, got out her battered laptop, and quickly logged in. Luckily she hadn't brought *that* into the Wynd with her. Her own phone, of course, was as long-gone as her anorak. "Contact your brother. Tell him to come get you at Lady Stairs. Tell him you'll explain the situation when he gets here. Ravi..."

She glanced around. He was eyeing the great stacks of paper cluttering every surface in the room and whistling under his breath.

She grimaced. This was why she hadn't wanted anyone up here. "Leave that alone," she snapped. At his wounded look, she forced herself to relax. "When Morgan's done I need you to contact every member of your support group. Let them know that Ram is an impostor, and that they mustn't come near the Royal Mile. Just because that creature isn't trying anything right now—" she glanced at the Eye again— "Doesn't mean that it won't again."

Questions tugged at her, but she couldn't address them yet. She had to come up with a plausible explanation for...well, everything.

"Nate's on his way," Morgan announced, hugging herself and looking grim, pale, and determined. Sky didn't blame her. She imagined her own face looked much the same.

Ravi got online and got to work. "They're going to want to come here, you know," he said, over his shoulder. "This is where Ram always said to go if we needed him. Lady Stair's Close."

*But it's not safe.*

Or was it?

Ram's protections, his powers, they kept this flat and the Eye connected and safeguarded. Perhaps the power reached further.

She had so much more to learn about being a Protector.

But one thing she *did* know.

Oh yes, suddenly, she knew.

Ram had chosen this place, this oh-so-central, recognizable, bustling place, for one reason: so those who needed him could find him.

She straightened her back and drew a deep breath. She still didn't know Ram's game. Really, she knew hardly anything at all.

But she was all the Lost Children had now. And she was bloody well going to be their Protector.

She'd be the Protector anywhere she needed to be in Old Town. And right here, in Lady Stair's Close.

# MARI LWYD

*Jennifer Lee Rossman*

We hear the bells first. Merry little jingles not unlike those on the merchants' carts, so far off and so faint that on any other night I would almost dare to mistake them for ringing in my ears.

But the stockings have been emptied, the turkey dinner reduced to soup bones, and we've all gone to Mass and filled our souls with holy superstition in preparation for tonight. It can only be the horse.

Dim light still fights its way through the heavy curtains. It's come early this year.

My sisters and I, frozen in place by the sound, share a look of horror, each of them no doubt sharing my hope that we'd imagined it all. That it was just some game our parents played along with, like Father Christmas. Then, in unison, we launch into action, our childhood duties surging back like muscle memory.

I race to snuff out the candles and douse the fireplace, running water over rags to dampen the smoke. Ffion goes to secure the doors and windows; a table scrapes against the floor as she blocks the kitchen door that never did latch quite right. And Alys is in the pantry grabbing the food and drink, along with Daddy's shotgun. It won't do her any good against something that isn't alive, but you try telling her that. The thing's been her security blanket since he taught her to shoot when she was seven.

We move with the practiced precision of a drill team, no footstep or second wasted, and it's only once we're locked inside in the near-darkness that I meet the children's eyes.

They look up at us from the floor where they were playing a board game. My little girl Serena, Ffion's son Luca, and Alys's boyfriend Harry. He might not be a child, but he's young and clueless and scared, so he's as much a liability as the kids are tonight.

Oh, Lord. I don't want Serena to grow up with this terror. Subconsciously, I think it's why I never brought her to see where I'd grown up until both my parents died—so they wouldn't goad the neighbors into playing Mari Lwyd again and scaring the living daylights out of her. But maybe they weren't playing.

I kneel on the floor beside the kids and hold my finger to my lips.

The bells grow louder, closer.

"Do you hear that?" I whisper, remembering the way Mum used to tell the stories. Like they were scripture, something to be awed and revered as much as feared. "That's the Mari Lwyd, and it's coming."

Luca looks to Ffion uncertainly as she goes to tape the curtains closed. "Mom?"

"Stay with your Auntie Caron," Ffion hisses.

Harry does the same with Alys as she drags a chair over to the front door and sits, gun at the ready. "Honey? What the hell's going on?"

Alys reminds me of Daddy when she grunts, "It's Christmas."

"The Mari Lwyd," I continue, taking Sarena in my arms as her inexpressible confusion turns to tears in that unique toddler way, "comes calling every Christmas. If it hears you, if it even hears your heartbeat, it sings at you, and you *have* to sing back. You have to sing better, cleverer songs, or it'll get angry and come in."

Luca's eyes are wide as the baubles on the tree. "What happens when it comes in?"

Alys checks the food beside her. It looks like everything from the pantry, but I know in my heart it won't be enough of an offering.

I look to Ffion to continue the story. She's the oldest, the only one who was born the last time the Mari Lwyd came in. When we were kids, she told us she remembered it, but how much of it was real and how much was invented memories is anyone's guess. I'm not so sure she even knows.

A long moment passes before Ffion says, "I wasn't always the eldest Bowen sister."

This sets off a flurry of questions and hushed shouts.

"Shut up; it'll hear!" The volume of my command startles even me, and I hold my breath in the abrupt silence that follows, my ears pounding as I strain to listen.

Footsteps. Not hoofbeats, but hard-soled shoes clomping softly on the cobblestones. Its gait is that of a human, the better to lull you into a false sense of security.

There's no way to tell how far away it is. The steps sound like they're right outside, but the bells still sound a ways off. I remember Mum telling us it's a trickster, that it throws its sound to throw us off.

Ffion comes to sit with me and the kids, treading lightly and avoiding the floorboards that squeak. She pulls her son onto her lap and holds him tight like Mum used to hold us on Christmas. I don't remember Mum ever looking so afraid.

This isn't right. We're the adults now. We're the ones putting presents in their stockings and drinking the milk they leave out. We're supposed to be the ones jingling the bells tonight, too.

We were supposed to inherit the mantle of Mari Lwyd just as we became Father Christmas. I never thought we'd still be cowering in the dark, afraid to breathe like we did when we were small.

A shadow encroaches on the curtain, the sharp silhouette of a horse's head. I turn Serena away, but my eyes are locked onto it.

The stories say it's not the entire head, just a bleached skull. They say it has unblinking, glass eyes that see into your soul. I don't know if they're right; I've been lucky enough to only see the shadow, but Ffion tenses beside me, remembering.

The bells are louder now, so loud I can't hear myself think, and underneath them is the sound of footsteps and rattling bones. I slide my hand up to cover Serena's mouth, praying she won't cry out.

I don't remember when I started holding my breath. My lungs ache, begging for oxygen, but I don't dare give in.

The Mari Lwyd has passed the door now, its silhouette patiently marching by the second window. Almost gone. Almost to the next house. Almost—

"This is so cool."

The bells stop mid-chime at Harry's whisper, plunging us into a silence so absolute it hurts, and the horse freezes in place.

*No.* I reach out and grab Harry's arm, digging my nails into his skin as a warning. Maybe it'll go away.

He jerks out of my grasp. "What the hell—"

"Shh!" Even the kids shush him. They know this isn't something to fool around with.

The Mari Lwyd turns, stares straight through the curtains. If it had the flesh to do it, its ears would be up and alert, searching for any noise.

Harry looks at us like we're being irrational, and goes to stand up. Alys swivels in her seat and aims Daddy's shotgun at him.

She won't shoot, won't even risk the sound of pulling back the hammer, but her eyes are dark and steady. She's not about to let her family get taken by a skeletal horse, and if that means she has to threaten to murder her boyfriend, so be it. I don't blame her.

For a second, it looks like the Mari Lwyd is moving on. Then the tapping starts, slow and steady, back and forth across the front of the house though the horse head remains stationary. Something like a broom scrapes against the door in long strokes. Ffion and I huddle closer; Alys cocks the shotgun.

That, more than anything else, fills me with a sense of doom. There's no use keeping quiet anymore. It knows we're here.

Still, I don't dare move, don't dare let myself cry. Mum never cried, so I can't, either. I have to stay strong for my family.

A low warbling comes from just outside the door, a song without words, without voice. The mournful whinny of the Mari Lwyd permeates the house, surrounding us until I can't discern its origin. It may be coming from the inside of my head, for all I know.

"This is ridiculous," Harry mutters, and that's the last straw.

I cling to the hope that we may still have a chance. It might not be singing at *us*. It might be singing at someone else's house, and will leave us alone if we can just stay quiet a little longer.

But I can't do that. I can't sit here and listen to someone tell me this isn't happening, that my childhood terrors are unfounded. I won't listen to him say smoke and mirrors are the reason I never met my big sister Efa.

"Stop it," I tell Harry, my voice shaking with the effort not to scream. "You stop right this second."

The Mari Lwyd delights in hearing us. Its bells ring louder, its song grows more insistent. The tapping at the door becomes a steady pounding, like the rattle of an epic windstorm.

It wants in.

"We need to sing at it," Alys says as the children start to cry.

We look to Ffion, whose horror I can see even in the dark. "It didn't work," she whispers. "Last time. We sang every song we knew. All the hymns, even Efa's silly skipping rhymes. It had heard them all before."

"You're going to *sing* at it?" Harry has to raise his voice to be heard over the chaos of the Mari Lwyd. "You think there's a demon horse out there, and your answer is to sing—"

The end of his sentence is cut off when the door slams open.

The Mari Lwyd stands there on its two legs, everything from its shoes to its toothy, grinning skull shrouded in a sheet that flaps and billows in the wind. Its eyes shimmer, glassy and unblinking, as it looks over the offerings at Alys's feet.

Alys trembles, Daddy's shotgun forgotten in her hands, and I pull her away from the door. Harry reaches out to comfort her, and something inside me snaps.

I give Serena to Ffion and stand, forcefully dragging Harry along as I march up to the horse.

Its breath is hot and smells like sulfur, but I don't flinch. That's what it wants: the fear. It thrives on it, on our desperation to satisfy its demands.

Well, I'm not playing along anymore. This ends here, tonight. My children will be the last generation to cower on what should be a holy night, and I only regret that I didn't do something about it when I was their age.

"I will not sing for you." I don't know if it can hear me over the bells and screaming, but I don't raise my voice. "No one in this house will sing for you ever again, nor will we feed you."

The Mari Lwyd lowers its head, glaring at me.

"If you want a sacrifice, take this one." I gesture at Harry, who yelps. I'm not actually planning to give him to it, but I won't cry if it calls my bluff. "We're done with you terrorizing us."

With that, I grab at the sheet covering it, and yank. The Mari Lwyd gives an awful shriek, throwing its head back and letting off a burst of heat that instantly melts the snow on the front walk.

The skull drops to the ground with a clatter, coming to rest beside its shoes, and a grateful silence overtakes the town once again.

The neighbors cautiously emerge from their houses. Someone grabs the skull and hangs it on a stick, and parades it down the street. I shut the door, taking care to lock it though I hope this is the last we'll see of the Mari Lwyd, and go to hug my family. We'll be back next year for the safe Christmas we always dreamed of, and we'll have a new story to tell about the Mari Lwyd.

# UNDER CONSTRUCTION

*Matthew Stevens*

"What do you mean it's gone? It's a roof on a building, it doesn't disappear." Real estate developer Harold Whithorn stomped back and forth across his spacious office. He paused to stare out the floor to ceiling windows at the activity in Boston Common.

Harold's personal assistant stood silently, arms holding a stack of manila folders to her chest, waiting for the phone call to end and to be acknowledged. She didn't take it personally, she'd worked for Mr. Whithorn long enough to understand by his tone whether she could interrupt the phone call or not. This was obviously not. She couldn't hear anything from the other side of the conversation. But, clearly, something was wrong. Absent-mindedly she tugged on her necklace, a small golden cross she'd worn every day since her confirmation, and whispered a prayer. An unconscious act.

"What about the cameras?" Harold paused for his answer. "What do you mean nothing? I don't pay for security cameras because they're pretty." His tone was inching past irritation toward fury. "Ok, so if the ones on site are worthless, have you checked with the church across the street? Certainly, they have security of some sort."

He stopped pacing. Never a good sign. His assistant took a step back toward the door.

Harold took a deep breath, moved the phone away from his face, and screamed at it. "What the fuck! What am I paying you for? I'll be there in twenty." He slammed the phone down.

With both hands flat on the desk, he took a couple of long deep breaths before turning around. "What do you have for me?"

She replied by handing him one of the folders.

He grunted. "Can this wait? Apparently, I need to go down to the Carney Park project and do other people's jobs."

"Of course, Mr. Whithorn. Should I leave them here on your desk?"

"Yes." His reply was terse as he pocketed his phone and made for the door.

♣

The drive to the building project took longer than Harold expected, which soured his mood even further. He punctuated his arrival on the job site with a loud slam of his car door. Within moments, John Taggart, the site foreman, exited the job trailer and made his way over to meet Harold.

"Mr. Whithorn, you didn't need to come down here. I was taking care of the issue," he began. Harold was well known among construction crews for his high pay and equally high standards. Along with those things came the possibility of being canned in an instant if the job wasn't progressing as he felt it should. So, Taggart stumbled over his words and his feet in an attempt to save face and, hopefully, his job.

Harold marched past without stopping to listen to the excuses pouring out of the foreman's mouth. "Apparently I did."

He came to a halt at the entrance to the unfinished building.

"Show me what's left and tell me how long it will take to catch back up," he said.

Taggart jogged up behind Harold. "That's the problem, Mr. Whithorn. It's completely gone. There's nothing left."

"That is impossible," Harold looked up to the unobstructed sky where just the day before the framing had been assembled for the roof. "Tell me you checked with the church for security footage?"

"Well, I, uh, tried."

"And what did you find out?"

Taggart wrung his hands. "They, um..."

Any patience Harold had left evaporated. "Did you find anything? Yes or no, dammit."

"No, sir. The cameras on the fence are for show."

Harold closed his eyes and cursed under his breath. Taggart made out one word, "Unbelievable."

"Assuming I can get the materials delivered today, we should be caught up in two days." The hint of optimism in his voice was shrouded in apprehension.

"I seem to be missing something here. Why do you have to wait for more materials? If the roof blew off, why can't you scavenge from that first?" Harold had started moving through the job site, as if searching for answers that were either missed or neglected.

"Boss?" Taggart paused.

Harold huffed in response.

"Because there isn't anything left. It's gone."

"Don't be absurd. That's impossible." Harold was almost laughing at the idea.

"I know it can't. The steelworkers and the carpenters agree. That's what's got us bothered. When you get up there," he gestured to the edge of the building where roof line met wall, "it's as if we never started connecting it at all."

Harold had heard enough excuses. It was like watching money float downstream, out of reach. "Fine. Do what you have to do, but I'll be back here in forty-eight hours, and I better see some progress on this God damn building or your job will disappear with the roof."

"You got it, Mr. Whithorn."

♣

Taggart greeted the semi-trailer with the roofing supplies bright and early the next morning at the gate. After the ultimatum, he'd slept in the job trailer. They unloaded the truck quickly, and everyone settled into work. He had no intentions of losing his job and his reputation due to some freak event.

By mid-afternoon that day they'd made so much progress that Taggart felt encouraged enough to call and let Mr. Whithorn know they were back on schedule. Right before 3:30, when the workers usually started wrapping up for the day, their supervisors marched into the job trailer.

They stood arms crossed, shoulder to shoulder. "We putting in OT today?"

Taggart walked to the window where he could see the building in progress. "How close are we to before the incident?"

Without hesitation, they all agreed. "Almost caught up."

"Good. Thank you and your men for their extra hard work today. Head out and we'll get back at it tomorrow, at a more usual pace," Taggart said, settling back behind his desk.

Once again alone, he leaned back in his chair, releasing a deep breath he'd been holding in all day. He scratched his head, still puzzled how all those materials could simply disappear without explanation. Taggart absently flipped through a couple of invoices and reports that lay strewn across his desk. His mind scattered like the pages of paperwork.

The sun began to dip behind the trees. To catch up and appease Mr. Whithorn was only part of the reason he needed that roof on the building. This time of year, construction slowed to a crawl if you couldn't work inside. New England winters could be rough and tended to be worse the less prepared a job was.

As soon as they finished the roof, the plumbers and electricians could get things moving inside. Mr. Whithorn demanded the building ready before spring. Easy enough, if the roof stayed on.

Before Taggart knew it, the sun had long set, shrouding the whole site in darkness. He couldn't shake the uneasy feeling he had about the whole situation. It was inexplicable. He had a sensation that something lurked outside the edges of his peripheral vision, waiting to be forgotten before emerging.

The cheap black and white clock that hung over the door ticked quietly and a rumble in his stomach reminded Taggart that it was time for dinner. To calm himself, he decided to grab a bite for dinner and buckle down in the trailer for the night. He could catch up on the rest of the work he'd shuffled aside in the craziness of the last two days. If he needed, the trailer had a couch—it was old and ragged, but for a few hours of sleep it would work just fine.

♣

Taggart shot upright on the couch. He'd dozed off. Blinking a few times, the clock came into focus. It was a little before three in the morning. He stretched as he rose, back and knees popping multiple times. Out of the corner of his eye he caught a flicker of light through the window. Probably a simple garbage truck on early rounds, but the raucous thumping typically accompanying garbage trucks was missing. It was too quiet. An eerie calm.

He stepped outside to investigate and spotted an odd yellow-white flashing through the copse of trees tucked beside the trailer. The silence followed him out of the trailer. The strange lights continued to blink in a pattern both random and but organized.

Not a garbage truck. The city, even this small corner, was never quiet, but right now not even the wind stirred. All at once the light grew and blossomed until Taggart had to shield his eyes. Across the street, high above, a single bell rang out from the church steeple. As quickly as they shone, the lights vanished, as if having been blown out. Subdued slightly, perhaps because it was overnight, two more low, long bongs rolled down the front of the church and over the job site. Three a.m. As the din of the bell faded into the night, the glow returned to the trees. Not as bold, not as intense, and in a sequence, but one whose meaning escaped the foreman.

In that same moment, to the right of the trees, closer to the newly constructed building, the fence gave a brief rattle. Taggart spun on the heels of his steel-toed work boots—not an easy task—and focused on the darkness shrouding the chain-link beneath the trees. The hairs on his arms and back of his neck stood up. Hidden in that gloom was something perverse.

The sodium lights around the job site were off after the crews left for the day. An unease that had buried itself in his gut begged him to turn them back on. Deep in the shadows he swore he saw two small dots of red, like raccoon eyes catching glints of light. In three sweeping strides Taggart reached the panel and threw the switch for the floodlights.

As the hum of electricity surged through the lines to each bank of lights around the site, a dim yellow glow immediately bathed the partially constructed building. It would take a few minutes for the lights to reach full power and illuminate all the blackened corners.

As an extension of his newfound paranoia, Taggart checked the padlock on the entrance gate before turning back to the building. On the far side of the building he heard a rustle and tiny snap like the shaking of a damp towel. He moved slowly, walking heel-toe, creeping.

At the edge of the building he stopped, listening. Down the length of the building came a series of noises that defied categorization. It sounded like a muted cacophony of grunts, cracks, rumbles, and groans. His brow furrowed with intense confusion but waited until the sounds stopped before peeking around the corner.

The glow from the lights continued to strengthen, chasing shadows back further. The bizarre silence that made Taggart feel uncomfortable returned, blanketing the entire job site. He took an extra moment to listen. Nothing.

With caution he didn't know he possessed he inched toward the corner, where the unfinished side of the newly constructed building came into view. In the distance he glimpsed an enormous black shape just as it disappeared around the back wall. He broke the quiet with an unintentional gasp. Part of him fought to break into a run and catch up with whatever he had witnessed while the more logical parts held his body in place, like a statue.

Across the site a crash of splintering wood cracked the silence, causing Taggart to jump. Common sense begged him to remain where he was, but his wallet and financial obligation to Mr. Whithorn forced him into action. The easiest path was through what would be the main entrance of the building.

Within seconds a tornadic wind blasted between the building and the job trailer. Taggart ducked his head as he pushed forward to the doorway. Over the thundering rush of air, a sharp whistle drew his attention, forcing him to raise his head. No sooner had he raised his eyes when a board came spinning at him, smashing hard across his nose.

Flat on his back, the world was blurry. An enormous black shape filled the space before him as he battled to focus through streams of red. Two smoldering coals floated in the center of his vision. A hot, putrid puff of air wafted in his face. Then a growl rumbled the ground, himself, the air … everything. After that, his world went black.

Taggart's eyes fluttered open. He sat up gingerly touching his fingers to the bridge of his nose. He flinched at the pain created by his own gentle touch. His eyes hadn't finished focusing when a voice from behind the desk drove a spike into his brain.

"What the hell happened?" Harold demanded.

Taggart winced, trying to keep his brain inside his skull.

Harold didn't give long for a response before a second assault, louder. "Well? I need an explanation."

Eyes still shut, he whispered a reply. "For what?"

"I swear, Taggart. Your ass is on the line here. Don't screw with me." Harold rose from the desk, scraping the chair against the floor, driving the foreman further into the couch. "When the other workers arrived this morning they found all the lights blazing, the trailer wide open, you laid out in front of the building with a huge cut across your nose and forehead, and the coup de grace…" He dragged another chair toward the couch and slammed it down. "The fucking roof. It's gone. AGAIN!"

If Taggart could have melted into the couch to escape the volume of Harold's verbal assault he would have. Instead, he was left cowering, hands clasped over his ears, begging to be left alone.

"Are you hearing me? I need to know what happened. Why is the roof gone?"

Taggart remained still and quiet as long as Harold would oblige. It wasn't long enough for the pounding in his head to subside, but enough that he could open his eyes and respond before being berated a third time.

"I stayed. Last night," he said softly, without sitting up.

His voice tempered, the developer prodded. "Yes, that is clear. But what happened?"

Taggart told what he recalled happening last night. To his surprise, Harold listened without interrupting.

Harold rose. "I'm going to make this simple."

Taggart sat, perched on the edge of the couch. He had a good sense of what was coming, but the tension was palpable, catching in his throat with every breath.

"I gave you a chance. An extra chance. And you fucking blew it. You're fired."

Taggart emitted a short, exasperated huff.

"Now, I'm not a complete monster. You will receive the standard severance as well as full health care until your injury—which I am legitimately sorry about—is completely healed. I do have one more request as your employer." Harold finally turned back to look at the dejected foreman.

"Yes, of course. And thank you." Taggart's shoulders fell.

"Order one final round of supplies for the completion of the roof. Then, head to the hospital and get that," Harold gestured at the wretched gash across Taggart's face, "looked at."

Without another word Harold left.

♣

Harold returned to the job site at the end of the next day to make sure it was progressing. The workers were wrapping up, and the materials had been ordered and delivered. After another day or two they'd be back on schedule. After the disastrous events of the past week, Harold decided that he would stay on the site himself and see if he could make sense of it all.

Without a new foreman, the desk in the job trailer drowned in piles of paperwork, none of which Harold knew how to complete or file properly. All he could do was sign off on the payments necessary to get the project built.

There was a knock on the door.

"Come in!" he called without looking up from the stacks of invoices.

The ironworker foreman followed his carpenter counterpart inside.

"Oh, good," he said setting aside a pale-yellow paper. "How close are we?"

The ironworker spoke first. "Close. We're gonna be behind because of this crap, but we're trying to make it up."

"Another day and we'll be where we shoulda been before this mess." The carpenter said echoing his cohort.

"Dammit. That'll have to be good enough."

The two stood silently for a moment waiting for further instructions. None came.

Harold mumbled to himself, shuffling papers back and forth across the desk as the foremen left. He was lost. Every word on the pages was like a foreign language, but he knew he needed something to keep him occupied while he stayed onsite.

He pushed the paperwork aside, pulled his laptop from his bag, set it on the desk, and started it up. He'd focus on organizing contractors for the next job across town.

Harold awoke with a shot, his knees colliding hard with the underside of the desk. A string of expletives filled the trailer. From outside he could hear the muted ringing of the church bell across the street. Then, in the quiet between peals of the bell came a noise. The fence bordering the site scraped and jingled.

A quick glance at the clock over the door indicated he'd only missed one bell, likely the one that had woken him. It was three in the morning, the same time Taggart claimed to have had his "experience." Harold yanked open the drawers of the desk, throwing things to the floor, digging for a flashlight. He found one on his third attempt and clicked the button a handful of times before bolting out the door into the night.

His feet hit the dirt. He rushed for the fence-line. To his left, tucked between the new construction and the street, were the few trees that hadn't yet been cut down. Buried deep within the branches from ground to sky, the tiniest of white lights blinked out one by one. Harold took a couple of small steps forward, his arm falling slack by his side.

Behind him, the metal of the chain link grated against itself. Startled, he loosened his grip, and the flashlight clattered to the ground. He nearly tripped over his feet trying to catch a glimpse of the source of the noise. Without taking his eyes off the fence, he retrieved the flashlight. In one motion he whipped it up and pushed the button to illuminate the barrier. Only, the darkness remained.

"Sonofabitch!" He cursed as he smacked the flashlight repeatedly against the palm of his hand, trying to force it into working order. Suddenly, the light came back on. The outside edge of the beam caught something. It looked like an all-black mop, but before Harold could fully process, it had vanished with the sound of a rug being shaken off.

The extreme silence that followed gave him the chills. Taggart had mentioned this eerie quiet. Even the regular ambient noises had disappeared.

Harold knew that he needed to try to locate whatever creature had wiggled its way onto the job site. It hadn't appeared big enough to cause significant damage, but God-forbid if it was someone's dog and it fell into a hole for a footing or knocked over a bundle of rebar and got trapped underneath. He would be staring down the end of a lawsuit before his secretary could stir the cream into his coffee.

To his right was the front of the would-be building. He swung the flashlight that direction. Even a full day of activity hadn't completely removed the stain of Taggart's blood from the dirt. His gut told him to listen for where the dog had gone, but his brain pulled him forward.

He hadn't gone two steps when the stillness of the night was disrupted by the whoosh of a breeze racing around the corner of the building. Riding with the wind came a low rumbling growl, freezing Harold dead in his tracks. He spun in a circle, whipping the flashlight back and forth, attempting to cover everything all at once.

As suddenly as the wind rose up, it stopped. The strange, still hush fell over the job site again. He crept forward to the uncompleted, open entrance. From inside the partially uncovered building came an unnatural series of grunts and cracks echoing off the bare unfinished walls. The hair all over Harold's body stood up as if pulled from his skin by an unseen force. He tilted the light beam, attempting to shine it all the way to the far end of the interior of the building. The light diffused long before it reached the source of those uncanny sounds.

Step by step he found himself inside the skeleton of the structure, the braces crossing over the top like ribs of a giant rotted carcass. He wasn't through the doorway more than ten feet when the gentle wind returned and immediately built into roaring gusts, drowning out the peculiar silence with the howl of tornadic winds.

The supports above creaked and groaned, fighting to stay in place against the push and pull of nature. The high-pitched whistle of the gale dropped octaves in tone as the speed increased. Then one by one Harold watched as the beams, braces and all, were ripped from the top of the walls. They crashed and thundered, snapping and splitting, wrenched into a whirlwind over his head.

Over the racket came the most gut-tightening sound he had ever heard. A deep snarl shook his soul, dragging his attention from the cyclonic disaster. There towering, over him, was the most frightening creature he could imagine. The shaggy, black, mop-like hair he'd seen in the edge of his light covered an enormous ogre-like beast. The only thing not covered in the fur was the head, where two coals burned with the fires of Hell. A short, almost snout-like nose was situated crookedly between oversized yellow-stained tusks. It opened its mouth, emitting a growl punctuated with dripping strands of saliva. Harold fought to control his fear. He stood statuesque, the slobber spilling onto his face.

The monster leapt over Harold and sprinted for the doorway behind him. Daring a glance upward, expecting to still see the swirling mass of construction materials, he was stunned to see only the dark blue of the sky sprinkled with stars.

He rushed to the front of the building, his eyes darting back and forth, begging to know where the creature had gone. The winds had settled down to a quiet breeze. Harold strained to listen. His entire body shook with a cocktail of adrenaline and fear. In the distance, a siren, followed by the honk of a horn, rebounded off the city. A city oblivious to what Harold had witnessed.

Past the job trailer he heard a groan of metal being forcibly bent. He reached the edge of the job site at an all-out run in time to watch the trees outside the fence wave and settle back into place. The support for the barrier had been twisted like a wet rag and the chain-link shredded like a napkin.

Whatever had been inside, whatever Harold had seen, was gone. Vanished. Then, for an instant, a minuscule star of light sparkled in the trees. Just as quickly, it disappeared. With the darkness came an overwhelming sense of dread. He couldn't put his finger on what exactly it was, but he knew, looking at the remains of the fence, that this project was doomed.

He could order all the trucks of materials, demand all the days of work, and they would never make any more progress. Never in his career had Harold failed to drive a job to completion, but this … was different. A force that he couldn't comprehend worked against him.

He walked to his Mercedes, which he'd parked outside the job site to avoid any accidental damage, dug through the glovebox for a fresh padlock to which only he had the key, rechained the front gate, and drove away. He'd call the crews in a few hours and let them know he'd find work for them elsewhere. The Carney Park job was permanently closed.

# JACE AND THE DAOINE SHI

*Tom Howard*

Everything Jace did upset someone. It wasn't his fault he was late.

"This is your fault," he told his shirt pocket as he ran down the narrow street to the big oak tree in the meadow at the edge of the village. "The sun's almost down!"

"Sorry," Az said, sticking his head out of Jace's pocket and clutching the fabric in his small green hands. "I'd just gotten to level thirty-seven on Dinosaur Wars."

"Hold on," Jace warned, jumping a pothole. His ten-year-old legs automatically navigated the familiar streets between his house and the Daoine Shi. Over the last two years, the fairy folk and he had become good friends, although Chief Myx didn't like the amount of time Az spent with Jace in his room. Lately, the old man insisted all of the Daoine Shi be in their homes by nightfall.

Chief Myx and a handful of the small green people waited at the clearing at the end of the street, sporting their tiny spears and wearing unhappy expressions. Jace couldn't recall seeing them carrying weapons or looking so unhappy before.

"I'm sorry, Chief." Jace lowered Az to the ground. "We lost track of time."

The old man shook his head, causing the dried grasses in his woven crown to wave. "These are dangerous times."

Jace knelt. "What do you mean?" The Daoine Shi were happy, musical fairies. He hoped they hadn't been harassed by the local kids.

"Is it another glitterball?" Jace asked. "I won't fall for that again." Jace had met the Daoine Shi when a specter looking like a bouncing ball had drawn him deep into the woods at the edge of town. The fairies, alarmed that a lost child, human or fairy, had been enticed into the dark forest, had revealed themselves to save him.

"Far worse," Chief Myx said. "It won't affect you, young giant, but something is out there, something deadly to the Daoine Shi."

"The starkling?" Az asked. "Has it been spotted?"

"What's a starkling?" Jace pushed his glasses up and looked for a threat in the lengthening shadows. He only spotted a gossamer carriage being pulled by two butterflies.

"A creature of darkness," the chief said. "Composed of trash, stones, and dead bodies, it grows and grows, searching for one thing."

"What?" Jace asked.

"Daoine Shi," Az said. He drew the slender sword he'd used playing Dinosaur Wars. "It feasts on us."

Jace frowned. "What will you do?"

"Find another meadow further away," Chief Myx said. "It's our only chance. It's too large to fight."

"Leave?" Jace's heart fell. "You can't." His battling parents had forgotten him. If he hadn't had Az and the Daoine Shi, he'd have run away long ago. "There must be a way."

"We've already sent patrols to find us a new location," Chief Myx said. "We'll leave this one soon."

"I should have told you earlier, Jace, that we were leaving. I'm sorry." Az hung his head.

Jace's friend would no longer be able to play Dinosaur Wars, nibble on pizza, or—

"What are you wearing?" Chief Myx asked Az. The young fairy wore a leather aviator jacket over the usual brown tunic.

"It's from one of my action figures," Jace said. "I gave it to him."

Chief Myx didn't look pleased, but he pointed at the sun, half hidden on the horizon. "We must go."

"See you tomorrow?" Jace asked.

"In the morning," Az said.

The chief nodded. "We can say our farewells then. If Jace is still able to see us."

"Why would I stop seeing you?" Jace asked.

"Because you're human and growing," Az explained. "Kids stop seeing Daoine Shi when they grow up."

"Even if we stayed," Chief Myx said, "you wouldn't be able to visit us much longer, Jace. You'd be unable to find our home or see us if we were standing in front of you. Your mind wouldn't accept it."

Jace didn't believe it. He knew exactly where the Daoine Shi lived. Cleverly disguised as a mass of braided and dried grasses, he'd lain nearby many times, listening to the beautiful singing of the Daoine Shi as they celebrated their festivals.

"I can help you fight the starkling," Jace insisted. "My dad has an axe in the garage. I'll get it and chop the monster up good." Never mind his father had told him not to touch the double-bitted axe.

"Too dangerous," Chief Myx said. "Just because you aren't its target doesn't mean it wouldn't kill you if you confronted it. Good night."

Jace fought back tears. Why hadn't Az told him they were leaving?

Az had recently discovered he could play Jace's video games without using a joystick. By pressing himself against the screen, he could transfer himself inside. He battled dinosaurs from within. He'd been so excited about his discovery, he'd probably forgotten to tell Jace the bad news.

Unhappy but unable to think of a solution, Jace stood. "Good night, Chief. See you tomorrow."

Never had the streets back to his house been longer. In the evening shadows, lights from the neighborhood houses seemed warm and cozy, but his heart was heavy. With Az and the Daoine Shi gone, he faced a lonely future. Jace had always been an outsider at school, a dreamer. He had no friends. Since the Daoine Shi had entered his life, he didn't need any.

Angry at life's unfairness, Jace heard china breaking as he slipped around to the back door. Soon, his father would storm to the pub. Once, Az had sung one of the Songs of Harmony while in Jace's room, and his parents hadn't screamed at each other for an entire day.

"You're so lucky," Jace had told Az, "being able to sing like that."

"Yeah, years to learn the fifty-seven songs to greet the morning, the hundred verses of Gurban's Saga, and the complete harmonies of celebration. It's almost as exciting as watching grass grow. Is there any pizza left?"

Jace entered his house. No one noticed.

♣

He woke late the next morning. Most of the night, he'd concocted ridiculous schemes to defeat the slithering pile of sticks that threatened his friends. Once or twice, the starkling had chased and caught him, adding him to the pile of decaying carcasses while the Daoine Shi fought and died around him.

The broken crockery from the night before had been swept up. He poured himself a bowl of cereal. In the summer, his folks didn't pay him much attention. Actually, they didn't notice him the rest of the year either. He hated his life.

He dreaded saying good-bye to Az and the Daoine Shi. Maybe he'd swing by the garage and pick up the axe.

His mother, looking tired, entered the kitchen in her bathrobe. On autopilot, she turned on the coffeepot and waited for it to brew.

"How are you, Jason?" she asked while her cup filled. "What do you have planned today?"

"The usual. Checking out the axe in the garage. Killing a monster."

"That's nice, dear," she said. "Do you want me to pack you a lunch?"

"No, Mom. I'll come in when I'm hungry. What are you doing today?"

"Your dad and I have an appointment this afternoon. You'll be okay by yourself?"

"No problem." He took his empty bowl to the sink and rinsed it. "You do know I'm ten, right?"

She smiled sadly and rumpled his hair. "I forget sometimes."

He slipped by her before she could hug him and start crying. She did that a lot lately.

In the light of day, Jace decided against the axe and headed for the meadow. On the street, the pungent scent of a dead animal hung in the air. Alarmed, Jace ran.

Az waited in the clearing beneath the overhanging boughs. He wore his aviator jacket, carried a spear, and looked worried.

"What's happened?" Jace asked.

"Something attacked one of our patrols last night," he said. "We can't find any sign of them. It had to be the starkling."

"I think I smelled it," Jace said. "Just now when I left the house. It's in town."

"Could you tell where?"

"No." Jace picked up Az and placed him on his shoulder. "It's a faint smell, drifting down an alley I passed."

"They can smell Daoine Shi," Az said, "but we've never been able to smell them. If it's hiding in the city, we'll find it."

"By ourselves?"

"Then we can tell the others where it is. Most of them are packed and ready to leave after last night anyway."

Jace smiled. "I have a better idea. Let's stop and get Dad's axe."

"Are you sure?"

"I can't sit and do nothing. We'll pretend it's a dinosaur. If it's too big for us, we'll run."

As they cut across another empty street, Jace stopped occasionally and sniffed the air.

"Anything?" Az asked.

"Seems to be getting stronger." In the garage, Jace lifted the large axe from the workbench. Heavier than he expected, he held it carefully. He shoved a nearby can of charcoal lighter fluid and a box of matches into his back pockets. If he couldn't chop it up, maybe he could set it on fire.

Something knocked over a garbage can on the street. "What's that?" Jace asked.

"They can smell Daoine Shi," Az said. "The starkling knows I'm here!"

Jace raced outside and stopped in the driveway. "I don't see anything."

"Look at the grass moving on the lawn," Az said. "It's coming this way! It's found me!"

"Don't panic," Jace said, swinging the axe. "I wish you were bigger. You're better with a weapon."

"Wait! I have an idea," Az said, standing in Jace's face. He placed his palms against Jace's glasses. "Say *shuis slo slumus sheen.*"

The boy almost laughed at Az's strained expression, magnified by his nearness. "*Shuis slo slumus sheen.* What does—"

Something popped, and Az disappeared.

"Az?" Jace asked. He searched the ground for his small friend. Where had he gone? Nothing moved on the lawn. The starkling had lost Az, too.

*Jace?*

Jace's vision blurred, and the colors surrounding him brightened. "Az? Where are you?"

*I'm in here. Inside you. Where it can't smell me.*

"You're inside me? Like the way you went into the video game?"

*Exactly. I wasn't sure I could. Are you okay?*

"Things look brighter, but otherwise, I'm fine." Jace hefted the axe. "Let's find it."

He strode to where they'd seen the grass moving, and at first, nothing looked out of place, but his human nose told him the starkling lurked nearby. Using Az's vision, Jace picked out a large clump of dead grass at his feet.

"I see it," he told his hitchhiker. The heavy axe felt lighter as Jace lifted it above the clump of dead grasses at his feet. He released it, letting the axe's weight bury it deep within the quivering mound.

It lurched. Jace stumbled back, but the axe had embedded itself deep within the creature. Worse yet, the wood of the axe handle had come to life and wrapped itself around Jace's wrist.

He fought the starkling as it pulled the axe, inch by inch, into its disgusting form.

Reaching into his pocket with his free hand, he removed the lighter fluid and popped the top open with his thumb. He emptied the contents onto the starkling as the axe continued to disappear into the creature.

He took out the matches but couldn't strike them one-handed.

"Az! I need you to come out and strike this match."

*But I don't know how to strike—*

"Just come out here!"

After another pop, his vision blurred, but instead of looking down at his little friend, he looked up at…himself! "What?"

"Strike the match!" Az shouted in Jace's booming voice.

"But the axe has us."

"Do it!"

Jace, standing on Az's giant palm, slid open the match box and extracted a wooden stick his own height. Dragging the match against the striking strip with both hands, he ducked when the heat flared up. "As soon as I drop it, try to pull away."

The glowing match floated down for an eternity, finally touching the starkling. It exploded in a flash of dry twigs and released a foul stench of decayed animals. It bucked and screamed.

Az fell backwards, released by the axe, but kept Jace safely in his fist.

"Watch out!" Jace shouted with his tiny voice. "The house is going to catch fire."

"What do we do?" Az scrambled to his feet.

"Go back into the garage. There's a fire extinguisher in there. It's a big red canister on the wall. I'll show you how to use it. Quick!"

Placing Jace in his shirt pocket, Az ran and grabbed the extinguisher.

"Pull the tab in the handle," Jace shouted. "Point the hose at the fire and squeeze the trigger."

Moments later, the unmoving starkling had become a pile of embers coated in flame retardant.

"What the hell are you doing?" Jace's father shouted as he came out the door, followed closely by Jace's mother.

Az dropped the extinguisher and scooped Jace into his fist. "Just burning some trash, Mr., Dad."

"Are you crazy?" his dad asked. He picked up the fire extinguisher and doused the surrounding grass. "Is that my axe in there?"

Peeking from between Az's fingers, Jace saw Daoine Shi poking their heads from the corner of the house. They must have come looking for Az.

His mother sobbed. "It's our fault, Richard. He's trying to get our attention. We need to tell him what's going on."

"There are going to be some changes around here, son," his father said.

Bending to tie his shoe, Az placed Jace on the ground with a wink. "Will there be pizza, Dad?"

To Jace, he whispered, "*Shuis slo slumus sheen* means 'mine is yours and yours is mine.' Do you want to switch back?"

Jace considered it, but he didn't want to be a human. He longed to leave the city and run free among the forests and meadows and sing with the Little Folk. Az, as a giant, might be more help to his parents. Jace would claim the starkling had knocked the harmonies out of him.

He'd have to learn them all over. If he tired of being one of the Daoine Shi, perhaps Az would trade back with him.

"Az, are you all right?" Chief Myx and the others gathered around Jace when his parents led Az into the house. "Is the starkling really dead?"

"Yes," Jace said. "We can to go home now." He hoped there would be singing to celebrate.

# THE BURNING OF THE BLUEBERRIES

*Hailey Piper*

The scent of burning blueberries brings me back through the years to my time with the Horned Brotherhood, its brush with something ancient, things that still haunt me years on. My senses of taste and smell dulled after the fire, but that scent stays. I first noticed when my wife tried to bake a blueberry pie and raw, ripe berries rolled onto a hot pan. Most people won't know that scent. I can smell them burning. They revive a memory so strong that I live it again.

It didn't start with the fire. It started with a dive bar. I seldom drink, my doctor says it conflicts with my medications, but it was my twenty-first birthday. There was no harm in going out someplace my friends didn't know about to have a moment to myself.

The bar was dim and smelled like its men's room. People weren't here to mingle. Depressing barflies clung to the barstools and even more depressing older men gathered in the billiards corner, desperate to attract a group of girls my age who were playing pool by themselves. Disgusting, but I didn't want to confront them and bring their attention down on me. I was more careful before the Brotherhood came into my life.

Then Marty approached the bartender and ordered a drink. He was the best-dressed of anyone in the bar, and to this day I have no idea why he stopped by that hellhole. Maybe, like me, he wanted to visit a place that his friends didn't know about.

He sat on a barstool next to me and said, "You don't belong here."

My shoulders tensed, the way they used to when a new person paid attention to me, but I shook hands with Marty anyway. I wasn't about to be clocked. "Where do I belong then?"

"That remains to be seen." Marty nodded to the corner billiards game. "What do you think of those guys over there?"

"I think they should find something better to do."

"What if I told you there's a place where a lot of men found something better to do than harass young women?"

Already I had a hunch he wasn't about to get involved in the corner situation, but the girls looked to be leaving. I flashed Marty a smile. Soon I would find out I'd passed a test I didn't know I was taking.

Marty was the assessor. "I think I know where you belong. Come along."

I should've been scared. Going to that dive bar was a bad idea, but so was leaving with him in a shared cab out of the city and into the green countryside. I spent most of the ride a nervous chatterbox who reminded himself that sometimes trusting a stranger is how people die.

But sometimes trusting a stranger is how people live.

Our cab turned off the dark road and onto the lengthy, curving drive of a pearl-white mansion. A bronze statue of a horned man stood at the center of the mansion's fountain, a fur cloak across his shoulders, hunting dogs at his sides, his face graven. The fountain water ran from a drinking horn held between his hands.

Marty paid for the cab ride and led me to the mansion's front doors. I might not have belonged in the dive bar, but surely I didn't belong here. At the time I'd never lived in anything nicer than a small apartment with four other people. The mansion could hold many more. Conversation rumbled from the far side of its double doors.

"Let me give you the tour." Marty pushed open the doors and led me into a palatial hall.

I had only seen places like this in movies, that massive stairway, the spacious parlor, grand halls that led to grander rooms. The men in conversation wore suits and drank from wine glasses. Elsewhere they sat on couches with beer bottles while a baseball game played across a television the length of my bedroom. Sometimes a man would break from what he was doing to clap Marty on the shoulder and say hello.

They paid no attention to me, yet. Mercifully.

"Is this some kind of gentlemen's club?" I asked.

"There's no kind of gentlemen's club like this gentlemen's club. We stand in the palace of the Horned Brotherhood."

The atmosphere was jovial. Marty showed me a billiards room that made the dive bar look like a pothole. There were rooms for video games, table tennis, card games, a grandiose kitchen, a gym, and much more, but the point was made before I saw even half of the mansion. The club's members wanted for nothing here.

It seemed too good to be true, and it was. But that came later, with the girl, and the secret.

"What do you think?" Marty asked me when the tour was done. "Interested?"

By then my legs were exhausted, but my face had frozen in an astonished grin. "I thought these kinds of places were more, you know, exclusive."

"Exclusive, yes, but to be homogenous is death." Another man appeared at the top of the second-floor stairs. He was older, taller than either of us, and he dressed in a burgundy suit.

Marty shook the man's hand. "Sir, this is Gabriel Jefferson, hopefully our latest recruit." Then he turned to me. "Gabriel, it's my pleasure to introduce Zachary Harvick, founder and leader of the Horned Brotherhood."

"A healthy brotherhood needs variety to survive," Zachary went on. "We don't exclude on race, nation, creed, or sexual preferences."

I couldn't help but think of the girls at the dive bar. "Only women?"

"You're bold." Zachary nodded to a nearby hall. "Women have their place here, and they're well-paid for it."

Imposter syndrome is a demon. At that moment it crawled up my spine and whispered evil in my ear, that every step of progress I had taken to be myself was written across my face, that I was transparent and found wanting, and I had brought it upon myself by bringing up women in a house of men.

But they didn't look at me that way. They looked expectant. They wanted me.

So I asked another question. "Then what's a man's place here?"

Zachary beamed. "Our one goal is to recapture the essence of the primordial masculine. The chase of beasts that lives inside every man."

"You have beasts to chase?"

He laughed. "In the woods out back. We have license to hunt year round." He went on talking about the yards, the outdoor activities, the festivities, meanwhile I was having a heart attack over dodging a bullet that had never been loaded, let alone fired.

Everyone there seemed so friendly. Even Zachary, for his oddities, had a sophisticated charm. All this pursuit of the primordial masculine, the chase of beasts—this is only normal man stuff, I told myself. I used my inexperience to rationalize away the bizarre. Too much, I found out later, but that first night I was enthralled.

It was four in the morning by the time I left the mansion. A brochure stuck out of my coat pocket all the way home, but I didn't need it. I knew that I wanted in. There were no dues. The Harvick estate provided everything. The exclusion of women bothered me, but the fact that I'd stepped right over that exclusion without question had a tantalizing allure.

To explain why this mattered so much to me at the time, before I learned the Brotherhood's secret, it's hard to describe. There's asking out a girl you like and having her say yes, there's entering the university you want, there's getting your dream job, but those aren't the same.

It's as if in that old existential parable when a man says to the universe that he exists, instead of dismissing him, the universe takes a closer look and says, "My God, yes, yes, you do exist. Congratulations."

That was how it felt to be invited to a gentlemen's club. It's not like I never had friends, but I did crave fellowship. This was affirmation. I could wave a membership card in my parents' faces and say, "Look at it! Read it! Men, exclusively, and I'm one of them!"

It wasn't about my parents. It was the exclusivity. They saw a man and said, "That's a man we want with us." Not just any man. They saw me. I belonged with them.

Every weekend became a holiday at Zachary Harvick's palace. I watched sports, took walks on the grounds, but most of my time I spent talking about anything, everything. I even let my guard down now and then, talked about how my parents and I were estranged, but never elaborated why. There were plenty of other men with their own family dysfunctions that they were more than happy to talk about. I soaked up every story. My confidence grew. I became a social chameleon who mimicked gestures and phrases without trying.

It was the first time in my life that I realized you could get drunk without a drop of alcohol. In the same way, my judgment was impaired.

I'd overheard at some point that there was an inner circle, men closer to Zachary than others, but those rumors didn't bother me. I was happy with what I had.

Then there was the girl. She was the first woman I saw with my own eyes in Zachary's mansion. I knew there were women who came and went from the rest quarters, but we didn't cross paths. This one was an accident. I had come in from the outdoors to use the restroom and forgot my way back.

After getting myself good and lost, I saw her leave a room down the hall, escorted by Zachary and two burlier men whose names I didn't know. She was trying to wipe tears off her face and wrap a white bandage around her arm at the same time. Zachary appeared impatient. The men led her away without noticing me. I didn't follow them. Instead I slipped into the room where they had come from.

A first-aid kit sat on the floor, open. There was a sink basin on one wall and a few chairs. The room was otherwise barren.

A door stood across from where I'd entered. It was wide, metal, carved with what must have been runes. Through the gap at the bottom, a draft tugged at my ankles.

I knew then I was risking expulsion from the Brotherhood even as I wrapped my hand around the doorknob, twisted it, and found it unlocked. I told myself this was no dangerous cult. These were the nicest people I'd ever met. I'd never felt better in my life, and now I wanted to ruin it for myself.

But it was the Brotherhood that put enough confidence in me to open the door. I was a man before I joined, yes, but by then I was the man they told me I could be. Had I been thrown back into that dive bar the night the older men catcalled that group of girls, I knew I would've said something.

I had to see the Brotherhood's secret. I had to know.

The door resisted at first, but that was only the draft from the other side giving me a hard time. It opened onto a dark stairwell. I wished I didn't have to be alone to descend those stairs, but Marty was elsewhere in the mansion, and for all I knew he was already aware of this basement. Maybe this, too, was normal man stuff.

I began the gloomy trek down the stairwell, but I didn't have far to go. The black stone walls beside the stairs soon spread to form the walls of a circular cavern. The floor below was soil. A golden sunlamp in the ceiling shined down on a tree at the center of the room.

It was a twisted, leaning tree. Its trunk spread thick as ten men and its limbs were leafless. I know precious little dendrology, but this was nothing native to the region. Even now, I'm not sure there are normal trees that can grow underground. But this was no normal tree, I soon found out.

There were no chains in the tree limbs. Nothing suggested the woman I'd seen had been wronged here.

Zachary's voice cracked the basement's silence. "If you're going to set foot on the soil, please remove your shoes. We're loose with the rules above, but this is a sacred place." He appeared at the top of the stairwell. Behind him stood the same two men who helped him escort the girl from the mansion.

For the second time, I feared for my life in the Brotherhood's mansion. No imposter demon whispered doubt in that basement. I'd seen too much of a powerful man's secret.

But Zachary descended the steps with a smile and clapped me on the arm. "That boldness does you wonders. I love your initiative, Gabriel. We normally wait a while before inviting a new member to the basement, but it's refreshing to see a newcomer reach down and grasp the crucial pillar of our establishment. You've discovered the Brotherhood's destiny."

The two men left us. We took off our shoes and socks and strolled the soil around the tree.

Zachary put an arm over my shoulders and I couldn't help but smile. Many times when I was younger I wished that my father would throw an arm around me that way, just dad and son, but even to my brother, who he respected, he was a cold man. Colder, now.

"The first night you came here, I told you about men's place in the Horned Brotherhood. To recapture the essence of the primordial masculine, to rejoin the chase of beasts lost on us in a softer world. I don't wish the world to change. Change is life. I want us to be reborn. What we do here, beneath the earth, will bring that rebirth."

He led me to the front of the tree, where it faced the stairs.

"I've been fostering this tree for twenty years, watered by blood and sweat and ceremony, and it's about to bear fruit. You saw the girl, didn't you? She was upset, but we paid her to be here, and she came of her own free will. We cut her, shallow, just enough of a scratch that she would bleed in the soil. We used to only scratch the surface, but so much time has passed that I felt I must've misread the ritual, that it needed the act of masculine violence to go a step further. It needed bloodshed."

"To do what?" I asked. I couldn't imagine a reason to pay women to be cut that wasn't some psychotic fetish.

"To summon the Masculine Aspect. A forgotten god of the old world." Zachary gestured along the trunk of the tree. "For every man with the steel to join us, we draw him closer. At the time of destiny, he will erupt from the tree and charge us with renewed strength, sharpen us as his weapons, and then don his true mantle as Master Huntsman. Then, the chase of beasts, forever. We will be made avatars of masculinity in the flesh. Renewal, restoration, and glory for the Horned Brotherhood."

I must've had a look on my face that I felt he deserved at the time.

"I know it sounds wild. It is! But it's also true. We're nearly there." Zachary pointed at my chest, where scars hid beneath my shirt. "We need bold men like you, who throw themselves at the new, to help my inner circle usher the Aspect into the world. Are you with us, brother?"

I told him I needed to think about it, the wisest decision I made that day. Zachary swore me to secrecy, as many in the Brotherhood weren't ready for this knowledge, and told me to come back the next day with my answer, as that Sunday evening there would be the next ceremony.

Out of his mind, I thought, desperate to dismiss Zachary's raving. The Horned Brotherhood was a front for cultists, its surface bounty a disguise for the bloodshed below.

Still, I couldn't dismiss the fellowship or the confidence that now belonged to me. When I went home to my little apartment where I looked in the bathroom mirror, I saw everything that dissatisfied me about my face. Right then I wanted to smash the mirror.

What Zachary said was normal man stuff, right? The chase of beasts. It's in our nature to be impatient, not to wait, but to pursue. I'm a man. I could be even more of a man. I needed to be as much a man as possible.

Yes. I was with them. They could still call me brother.

I returned the next day with my answer. That night, I gathered in the basement with about fifty other brothers, the inner circle. Marty was among them and gave me a nod. Then we began the first of many rituals and ceremonies.

Most of it was harmless. We wore robes of earthy greens and browns. We sang songs in a language I didn't know, led by Zachary as he read from a book with a wooden cover, its surface knotted, with runes carved into the wood. They would pass around a drinking horn filled with wine that tasted like blueberries. I could skip out on any drink I wanted on the surface, but down here was a sacred place. They placed it in my hand. I told myself just that little sip wouldn't be enough to upset the antidepressants and hormones.

They were lies. I was sick the next day. Had I suspected then that it had nothing to do with my medications, that there was something special about the blueberries in the wine, something meant to prime us for the coming ritual, would I have left? I don't know. I found as many excuses to leave as I could, and then ignored them.

If a knife in my hand couldn't make me leave, nothing could. I just kept telling myself that the girls were being paid, they came to do this willingly, that we kept our instruments clean and ensured their wounds were superficial, that they were treated with respect. It didn't make the bloodletting any easier. There were still tears in their eyes and mine as well.

I asked Zachary how long this had to go on before the summoning of the Aspect.

"We plan to be ready by the spring equinox. Yes, that close. There's some debate among the brothers as to whether the date is important or merely ceremony."

Marty cut in. "Only ceremony. Our actions are the catalyst."

While the practice of these rituals was respectful, the reception afterwards was as jovial as the usual mansion activities. The rest of the brothers remained oblivious and the inner circle happily joined in their usual fun. They either believed we were on the right track or took the rituals as a silly requirement to join the most trusted clique in the Brotherhood.

That I didn't ask any of them what they thought says where my feelings were headed. Enough sickness after drinking from the horn made me wonder if something was wrong. I kept my guard up now because I didn't know who was buying Zachary's plan and who was laughing along for the ride. I was losing the bonds I'd formed. More important, I didn't want anyone to know I doubted, and if we weren't supposed to believe it, I didn't want to look like a fool.

I certainly felt like one. The more times I saw the basement tree, the more I became sure it was dead. How couldn't it be dead? It was planted underground with only a sunlamp for photosynthesis and watered only by scant drops of blood. Zachary was unhinged, and I was unhinged for joining him.

But the more I convinced myself that the tree was dead, the more I felt it staring at me. Not alive, but conscious. Aware. It took another handful of visits for me to understand why. The tree didn't matter, really. Dying, dead, irrelevant. We weren't feeding the tree.

We were feeding what grew inside the tree. That was the presence I felt.

From that evening on, I made sure I wasn't the last one out of the basement at the end of a ceremony. Still, I felt the tree watching me. Even above, it lingered, as if its roots crept through the mansion walls.

One night I dreamed I was in that stairwell, and I wasn't alone. I carried a heavy axe at my side, its blade glinting beneath the artificial sun. I kept my shoes on. The axe and I strode across the soil to the trunk of the tree, and we hacked at its front, hacked it open to kill whatever grew inside, kill it in the womb.

It was an idea. I didn't plan to do it, but I thought about it until I visited the basement the next Saturday, where a vertical crease had formed from the base of the tree trunk and up past my height.

"We're nearly there," Zachary said. "The night of the equinox, be ready."

I would have to be. It was too late to stop it. Cutting the tree open would only help the Aspect into the world, premature but still here.

Only now there was that crease to stare at me for the next five weeks. It taunted me like a mirror. "You won't leave," it seemed to say. "You want to see what's going to happen. You want to change. That's why you'll stay. You'll do everything they want you to do."

I told Zachary I was concerned. What if we performed the ritual and felt no stronger inside?

He gave me a friendly jostle. "It won't happen just on the inside, Gabriel. We're not conjuring up a good feelings placebo. We call to the Master Huntsman. He'll sharpen our hearts, true, but he'll sharpen our bodies as well. Be patient. The strength will come."

I was not comforted. Anxiety tightened my nerves as each day brought the ritual nearer.

Even after everything, I could've left, no strings. The Brotherhood wouldn't keep me against my will, though Zachary would've tried to talk me out of it.

I never gave him a reason. Despite my anxiety, I was captivated by the possibilities. Science is imperfect. It always will be. Imperfect and limited, and I can testify to that as well as anyone. All the hormones and surgery in the world have limits. Maybe it isn't like this for everyone like me, but I was always told to keep my expectations in check.

This mysticism, this frightening divinity, the destiny of the Brotherhood, to inherit the Aspect—that was beyond expectation. That was euphoria. Maybe I didn't have to see limits. Maybe I could be like everyone else.

So even as I shed blood for them, sang their songs, sipped from their horn that made me sick at night, even as my nerves rattled every time I looked at that twisted tree, I stayed. Through to the bloody end, I stayed. I wanted to see a miracle.

On the spring equinox, I did.

It was a chilly night. Only Zachary's inner circle gathered at the mansion. Fifty of us put on our robes and descended the stairwell like usual, but the basement had changed. Torches lit the ring of soil.

The torchlight played with the crease in the tree trunk. It seemed to flicker and slide, as if its shape and depth were inconsistent from moment to moment. Something stirred within.

Zachary stood before the crease, and I fussed with my robe close by. Whatever came through that opening, I would be among the first to see it.

"The Masculine Aspect is prepared," Zachary said. "The tree will be split asunder as he storms forth into our world. What blood must be shed has been shed. What time must be spent has been spent. Our sacrifices are complete. Tonight we inherit our reward." He opened his wooden book. "If you will all repeat after me, we will sing the war cry as befits the Master Huntsman so that the Aspect may assume the form which best suits him, and so we will assume the forms that best suit us."

While Zachary found his page, I wondered what ways this might go wrong. The Aspect could be enraged for having been brought here. It could change us into things we wouldn't like. It could kill us.

Zachary began to sing, one line at a time, so that the Brotherhood could sing after him. This went on for what felt like an hour. I wasn't ready to see what emerged, and at the same time I was impatient to get it over with.

We had barely finished the last syllable when a heavy wooden crack echoed through the basement. I couldn't see an opening in the tree, not right away, but on the inside it was coming apart. Another rich crack and I spotted a slight gap at the top of the crease. The Brotherhood held its collective breath. I leaned forward, ready.

The crease split open from top to bottom, a seam being spread apart with threads of weeds between the sides. Golden sap slid down the edges of the wound and a green arm of pulp and leaves stuck out from the tree's inner darkness.

"Do we help him?" Marty asked.

"Let him come his way," Zachary said.

The green pulp slithered off a slim arm. Fingers grasped the tree by its wound and pulled a form through, covered in green vines. The vines grew like hair from a green scalp, so long that they could cover the figure if she wanted. Her slender form crawled from the tree on trembling legs.

She hunched then, but if she had stood tall she might have crested Zachary's height. Roots and wiry plant matter sprawled from her backside, an umbilical cord still tied to the insides of the tree. Across her body grew small canes of blueberries and their leaves. Many of the berries fell to the soil as she took her first steps.

The mass of hair-like vines looked us over, and then the face emerged. The forehead wore the same texture as Zachary's book, a knotted and aged chunk of ancient tree. Plates of similar bark crept across the shoulders, the joints, and along the chest and thighs. She looked something like a human girl, something like a deer, all made of greenery. Her expression told me she was confused, as if she had left a party and had no idea where she'd parked her car. Probably all of us looked confused.

Her enchanting eyes, blue as the blueberries that dotted her body, caught me in her gaze. We were lucky to be there in that basement. She was the miracle. That was all I could be certain of. The tree had given birth to something that was not the Masculine Aspect. I didn't know what she was, born of that ancient tree. I'll never know. Zachary didn't know, either.

There was a chorus of questions much more passionate than when we recited his mysterious songs. Who was she? Where was the Aspect? The Master Huntsman?

Zachary licked his fingertips and turned pages. Lightning slid between the brothers and through my nerves.

Maybe the green woman was the Aspect in an unsuspecting form, I wanted to suggest, but I kept my mouth shut. I knew it wasn't true.

Zachary fumbled with his book. "Perhaps I mistranslated." He turned another page. "The bloodshed of women—the blood shed by man. It's difficult. Their use of pronouns and past tense wasn't the same as ours. I may have misinterpreted the action's significance, but the blood we shed being women's blood—" He lost his words and retreated from the tree.

The lightning between brothers grew forked and spread in all directions. It cooked the air with broken promises.

I expected better from Marty. He ripped the wooden book from Zachary's hands and tossed it at the tree. It struck the green woman on the shoulder and fell softly on the soil. He might as well have thrown down a gauntlet.

The Brotherhood's rage awoke. They started shouting all at once, some of them at Zachary, others at the green woman. I slumped down and covered my ears. They weren't angry with me, I told myself. They were angry at the mistake and their expectations. I told myself these things in my head, over and over, desperate to drown out the violent roar.

I couldn't drown out the scream. Or the smell.

Did Marty start it? I didn't see. Someone grabbed a torch from along the ring and threw it at the twisted tree, where it landed among the roots. A thick tree like that would take a long time to burn. The green woman fell on all fours and clawed at the earth, but the soil here was shallow, an illusion to soak up years' worth of blood. There was nowhere to go.

Zachary grabbed the next torch. Maybe he thought that when the Brotherhood finished with the green woman, they would turn on him if he didn't show he was one of them. And he'd had his expectations shattered as well. He was an old man. Likely he expected the Aspect to return him to his prime.

Would they turn on me if I didn't start hollering and crying for blood? If I didn't show I was one of them? There were a few who stood silent, but none of them looked as horrified as I felt.

Zachary threw his torch. It hit the green woman and fire flared across her left side, along the vines and blueberry leaves. Her scream hurt my ears. Some of the men's shouts grew louder while others started cheering, all of them still angry. Zachary was giving a command. I couldn't understand him. There was too much noise and she was burning. I couldn't see clearly through the tears in my face, only the green shape and the yellow-white glow that ate at her side. That cacophonous basement was burying me.

I added to the din, another growling, shouting scream among fifty other growling, shouting men. Maybe they didn't hear me, but they saw me. I charged across the soil, ripped off my robe, and threw it across the green woman in a tackle. We collapsed into the soil together, where I patted at the flames to put her out. The smoke clouded my face and hurt my eyes, my nose, my throat. It had the smell of burning green twigs and blueberries in a campfire. I fought through the stinging until there was only smoke, no fire.

"Gabriel?" That was Marty. I didn't answer him. Zachary might have spoken next. The other men were still shouting, as if the Aspect had come to the Horned Brotherhood after all and filled them with blinding fury.

The green woman was whimpering, meek, scared, and weighed light as a small tree branch. That was good. We were leaving. They could chase me, but I was taking her away. I picked her up in one arm and she latched herself around me. Then I started to walk. Her tether snagged between us and the tree.

The Brotherhood closed in. If they suspected anything different about me then, I'll never know. They saw I wasn't one of them and that turned a knife in their guts. I didn't have the ceremonial knife on me, nothing to defend us. So, I tugged. And tugged. If I'd realized then what I was about to set in motion, I wouldn't have done any different.

Zachary didn't know the half of what he was playing with, how the tree was exactly what he said it was in ways he couldn't understand. The pillar of the Brotherhood.

I tugged one more time, which pulled the green woman loose. The tether of roots snapped back and sank into the tree. I felt the way I did the last time I went to an amusement park and the roller coaster crested the top of the hill, that sudden weightlessness, somewhat sickening, and then a plunge.

Chunks of black stone collapsed from the wall behind the tree. Everyone stopped to look, even me. On the wall where the chunks had broken loose lay a thick, scrambling layer of roots.

Another chunk of stone fell, this time from the ceiling, and it landed in the crowd. Now the men were screaming and panicking as the roots sank and the basement pulled itself apart.

When the sunlamp went out, I charged through them. The stairwell was short, and I was the only one with a firm direction. Everyone else was busy stumbling over each other in the dark. They had no purpose, while I had to get her out of there.

I found light at the top of the stairs and through the secret door, but no safety. A black fissure ran across the wall. The basement held up the center of the house, and if the basement was collapsing, the house was, too. I darted out of the side room, through the halls, desperate for an exit. Front or back, I didn't care.

A wall came down ahead of us before we reached the back door. I had to turn around and rush through the dining hall, where the floor sank to my left. Then through the parlor, past the stairs that imploded alongside me, and at last out the front double doors, into the parking lot.

The green woman clutched tight to me. She never tried to get away, never acted like I might hurt her, though she was wrapped in the uniform of the madmen who wanted to burn her alive.

There was a rumble outside, but I didn't wait to see who might make it out behind me and I didn't call a cab. I just kept running. The foundation of the mansion was a mystery to me and I had no idea whether the parking lot, the driveway, the horned man fountain, any of it might fall with the chain of dominos I'd set in motion when I pulled the green woman free.

I don't know when I slowed down. The run was hard and my shoes were buried in the mansion's basement. I think we made it to the dark road that turned off to the mansion's curving driveway before my legs realized we were safe. The city was a distant glow then, many miles to walk. I didn't have a plan except to get far enough away from the Horned Brotherhood so that it was like I was never there. Eventually there would be police, ambulances, fire trucks. I didn't want to have to answer any questions.

We didn't speak. I only noticed something was wrong with the green woman, besides her burns, when I tried to sit down after a while. At first I thought she wouldn't let go. Then I realized she couldn't. Her limbs had sprouted small digits from where the tree bark covered her green flesh. She was trying to take root in my clothes.

I pulled her away and let her roots rip at my jacket, shirt, and pants. My clothes made out better than Zachary's house. A little ways off to the side from the dark road, I laid her down in the crabgrass between two pine trees. She made a soft sound, almost purring.

Nestled firm in the soil, she closed her eyes and grew still. I sat with her and waited to see what would happen, but nothing did that night. What I knew for certain was that she was gone. I think she went back where she came from, to a long sleep inside the earth after having been briefly awoken by ignorant mortals. That's what I hope. We were only together for a couple of hours and most of it we just wanted to survive. I spent the rest of the night walking home.

That weekend I took a cab ride out toward the mansion in the effort of keeping up appearances only to find the driveway blocked by yellow tape. The news had reported the collapse already and spread it across all kinds of media. There was an obituary for the late Zachary Harvick. There were going to be many more obituaries and many more funerals for all the deaths at the mansion. Many of them deserved it.

There were a lot of people in that basement, and most of them died. We were all men down there. I had a chance to become like them. Instead, I was the only one who saw a wrong and did something about it, and that alone makes me bigger than any of them.

On the way back, I asked the cab driver to pull over. I needed to check on the green woman. If anyone else found her here, I didn't want them to hurt her. I had to make sure she was hidden.

There was no need. The plates of bark that covered parts of her skin had overtaken the whole of her, so that now she appeared as a length of womanly tree root that jutted between the two pines on the side of the road.

When I visited again weeks later, I found her covered by a flourishing green bush. Long green canes shot in all directions, overgrown with sweet, plump blueberries. If anyone disturbed her, it would only be to pick this fruit. She was safe deep in her earth.

# BANSHEE

*Serena Jayne*

The neighbors claim not to hear anything otherworldly over the domestic squabbles and traffic noises that breach our thin walls. Yet each night I wake, covered in sweat, heart thumping, pulse racing; ears ringing from the ghostly woman's wailing. Her declaration of doom and death.

No longer confined by my dreams, she's everywhere. Isolating myself within a crowded city to contain my crazy, I summon the courage to look closely at my tormentor.

Long inky hair. Shadows under her eyes. Red rosebud lips open wide in an endless scream.

No one I care for is safe, because she is me.

# FRAGARACH

*R. J. Howell*

"Fetch you *what?"* I sputtered. My voice echoed off the tile walls of the Resurrection Hospital morgue. Of the three of us present, I was the only corporeal one and, as such, my voice was the only one capable of physical interaction with our surroundings in the cutting room. "You can't be serious!"

The ankou grinned. It was wearing my dead brother's form again, dressed in the same old ragged jeans, black t-shirt, and jacket Kennett had worn on the night of his death, and the expression was a mocking imitation of Kennett's humor. On Kennett, that smile would've made me groan, anticipating another brilliant idea that would somehow end up with me on the other side of Chicago, fifty dollars poorer, trying to hogtie a gutted mattress to the roof of my car. On the ankou, it just left me suspicious and a little sickened.

I glanced over at Teddy's ghost to my right. He was still faded slightly at the edges, that blurring that most recently severed spirits suffered from, but his core essence had strengthened in the last few minutes since the ankou had bound him to my curse. He wore a pair of gray pajama pants, a t-shirt dotted with holes, ragged slip-on shoes, and a parka, all an exact copy of what his corpse in the chiller room now wore, though sans the blood and dirt.

For sixty-two-year-old Theodore O'Byrne—or Teddy, as he insisted I call him—had taken his dog for a walk and never returned home. The victim of a hit-and-run, he'd died en route to Resurrection.

His ghost, for the most part, had been more concerned about the safety of his dog than the fact that he was dead. After confessing I didn't know his dog's fate one way or the other, he'd fallen silent, and remained as such right through the ankou's manifestation. Which was rather impressive; the ankou was anything but subtle.

Teddy's eyebrows rose in a silent shrug. Clearly, he wasn't going to be of any help.

I turned back to the ankou. It lounged against one of the steel examination tables, its legs crossed at the ankle, its fingers tapping the surface in silence. "You can't send me on a quest to find a *mythical* sword. I can't complete that task! That's a violation of the bargain!"

"It is not myth, child."

"Bullshit!" The ankou was setting me up for failure. So it *hadn't* forgiven me for my previous—if accidental—violation of the bargain, robbing me, had I succeeded, of the initial two hundred and thirteenth completed task, putting me one step closer to the end of my sentence, and the ankou of a potential soul had I failed.

"It is not myth. *Fragarach* has been passed one hand to another, from Manannán to Lugh to Cú Chulainn, onward and downward through the ages, from deity to mortal to everything in between, and when one sword could no longer hold the full idea of *Fragarach*, it splintered into pieces to better encapsulate itself."

"It's a magic, mythic sword. Magic, mythic swords *do not exist.*"

"*Child—*" The ankou tipped its head back, rolling its eyes in a fair imitation of my brother's familiar drama. That old, aching hollowness in my chest gave a kick. My brother, my little brother… I refused to blink, refused to give the tears a gap in the shield-wall around my grief. Forced myself to stare at the ankou till that ghost of Kennett faded, and the only thing left was a being older than comprehension and masterful at holding grudges. "Claymore Atwater, you are a magician. You *know* that magic is truth, that the inward grain of the world controls all, that I am what I am, and yet you question whether *Fragarach* exists?"

"Magic, mythic sword," I said, quieter this time. "Forged by Irish gods."

The ankou tipped a hand from side to side. "Yes and no. The original, true *Fragarach,* yes, but as per the stipulations of your punishment, I may not give you so difficult a task as bringing me the true *Fragarach.* I will settle for one of its many splinters."

"Right. Of course. And how the hell am I supposed to find a splinter of a mythical sword within ten hours?"

"If it were not possible, I could not give you this challenge." The ankou made a point of looking up at the clock hanging over the swinging doors that led out to the hallway and offices. "And it's technically nine hours and forty-eight minutes, as you have wasted a fair amount of time complaining and asking pointless questions."

I scowled. Hardly pointless, and it wasn't *complaining,* it was expressing justifiable outrage and frustration at being given a task so ridiculous-sounding as *find me a mythical sword.* Magic was one thing. Magic was real, magic sang through my blood, imbued my every step with a resonance that echoed down through the depths of the earth and along the arteries of the world.

Mythical swords, not so much.

"And how exactly am I supposed to recognize a splinter of *Fragarach*?" I asked, struggling to keep my tone curious instead of exasperated.

The ankou made a soft *hm-hm* noise. "Oh, there is no mistaking it. You will know its bearer and its vessel, even if it is currently sheathed and hidden from the eyes of the world. Its name is inscribed upon the blade."

I frowned. "That's a contradiction. If it's sheathed, I can't damn well *read* anything written on the blade, can I? And, while we're at it, is this a literal splinter or a figurative one? Am I looking for an actual *sword*? And is the bearer and the vessel the same thing? Or are they two separate entities?"

"If the answers were so easy to give, it wouldn't be much of a task."

"I'm asking for ground rules and definitions!"

"Bah! Cheating!"

In my periphery, Teddy's hand slowly rose. "Um. I think you're looking for my niece."

I—and the ankou—stared at him till he, just as slowly, lowered his hand and did a silent imitation of a guilty shuffle. "I mean, we don't really talk about it but, um, she does have a sword. Kind of. I mean, it isn't a *real* sword, it's a tattoo on her back right over her shoulder blade but, I mean, it has that word you keep saying written on it. When she'd said she was getting a tattoo, everyone just kinda, you know, assumed she was going to get something girly like a rose or a heart or something, but then she came back with this giant sword. Which, I mean, I guess makes sense, she does do a lot of medieval sword fighting and reenactment stuff, and it does look nice. For a sword, you know. And you can't really see it or anything unless she's wearing a swimsuit—"

The whole thing felt like an uncomfortably familiar situation, one that had bitten me in the ass before. Humans, see, were next to impossible when it came to fetching. They never were where you expected, rarely went where you needed them to, and almost never kept to the ankou's timetable, especially when you sound like a madman babbling about magic and ghosts and curses and Breton mythological death figures. *Shit.* "New terms of the bargain! If the vessel is human, you come to me when I find it, and the presence of the vessel counts as the sword. I am *not* ripping a sword out of a person, if that's what you want."

"Mmmm, you ask too much, child. I will agree to your first term but as for the second..." The ankou's eyes closed and its expression smoothed into one of placid deep thought. Its lip twitched. "I think not. The sword *must* be manifest. How that is brought about is up to you. And I swear upon your curse, I will not claim *Fragarach* in any way for myself nor does the task explicitly require you to harm the vessel. However, if you cannot make the blade manifest itself without violence, that is not my responsibility." The ankou jerked its chin down in a firm nod. "You have nine hours and forty-six minutes."

With that, the ankou's form folded in on itself, dissolving into the shadows that spawned it and, with a final shriek of a steam whistle, the thundering *tu-thump tu-thump tu-thump* of heavy wheels on an uneven steel track, the deafening roar of a passing train, it fizzled away into nothingness.

I turned to Teddy. "All right, look. If I don't find what the ankou wants, your soul is forfeit. No, I don't know what the ankou does with souls, and it lies to me almost as often as it tells the truth, so I don't trust anything it says about the matter, but I do know if I don't complete the task, you will, essentially, go caput. Clear?"

"Yeah, though I don't understand why I'm getting the short end of the stick here—"

"Because the ankou is fae, and fae don't understand fairness. They can be equal, they can be just—though their justice tends to be violent, gruesome, and occasionally vile. The ankou has bound you to the bargain, and I'm sorry, but it just is. Now." I pressed my hands together as if in prayer and tapped the tips of my fingers against my lips. "Your niece. How would I go about finding her?"

Teddy crossed his arms. "Only if you promise to find Benny first."

Teddy's dog. "I swear, I will find out what happened to your dog," I said, not making the mistake of saying that I would *find* his dog nor in what order I would complete either task. I'd had far too much experience with the fae and the binding nature of promises.

Teddy frowned at my word choice—or, perhaps, just frowned in consideration—but agreed in the end.

Find *Fragarach* and find the dog, all in less than ten hours. Oddly, both of these requirements coincided with the finding of Sandy O'Byrne, the only member of the extensive O'Byrne family currently living within the city limits of Chicago and, thus, Teddy's nearest next-of-kin.

Sometimes, working in a morgue as a magically-inclined pathologist has its perks. Access to certain medical and governmental databases, along with Google and Facebook, was one of them.

Cassandra 'Sandy' O'Byrne, thirty-two, was a member of the SCA—or Society for Creative Anachronism—and a regular employee and actor at the Bristol Renaissance Faire up in Wisconsin during the summer. In the mornings and early afternoons, she worked as a barista at a Starbucks; in the evening, she offered classes at her local YMCA in saber and épée and, once a month on a Saturday, lead workshops with her partner in stage combat.

In short, Sandy O'Byrne was a swordmaster. Fitting *Fragarach* would choose her as its wielder. Or, as the case may be, its vessel.

Unfortunately, tracking her down had to wait till I finished my shift, during which I prepared Teddy's body for autopsy, conducted the preliminary exam, did intake for a—mercifully unhaunted—deceased woman who'd died in the hospital of apparent kidney failure, and, in my spare time, synchronized the resonance of Teddy's blood with the vial of my own that I carried around my neck for that purpose. A blood-based tracking charm, it functioned more like a dowsing rod than the traditional scryer's crystal and map. Though it couldn't tell me exactly where Sandy O'Byrne was, it could indicate where she wasn't so my hunt became more a process of elimination.

Though I ducked out an hour early at four, I had still lost a precious three hours and some minutes along with most of the daylight. During the winter in Chicago, even in late November, the sun started sloping toward sunset around three-thirty and by four had mostly sunk behind the sprawl of the West Side, the sky a pale silver-blue over the Lake fading overhead down into pink and orange. A clawing, icy wind tugged at my hair, sliced right through my coat, and I hustled over to my SUV, a black Toyota sliding steadily from gently used to old but reliable.

Teddy had followed me out and, after staring at the door for a good long minute, phased through and took his place in the passenger seat. I considered the benefits versus cost of having a remote start installed, and that kept my mind busy for the five minutes it took for the engine to warm up enough to turn the heat on.

And so began my hunt.

I'd meant to cast the net as wide as I feasibly could given the deadline, planning to center my eight-mile-wide circuit first on Sandy's apartment in the north end of Cragin, then the gym in Old Irving Park where she taught saber on Wednesday nights, but the keyed vial of blood around my neck pulled me back to the northwest. Toward the hospital. Toward Teddy's body? But, no, I'd keyed the spell to look for *living* blood, not the dead.

Frowning, I turned and followed the pull. We passed Resurrection Hospital and kept going northwest down Talcott. The sun sank lower, the blue of the sky deepening.

"Do you know where you're going?" Teddy asked after almost ten minutes of snaking and weaving my way through side streets, waiting for the resonance to begin to fade before turning down the next street, then the next.

I shrugged. "Sort of."

"Really? Hm." Teddy went back to staring out the side window. The resonance faded again, and I hung another left, completing the latest in our series of giant rectangles circling the source of the hum.

"This is my neighborhood, y'know," Teddy said. "You'd think it'd look different. When you're dead. Like, sadder, somehow." He sighed. "Never finished raking up the front. Meant to get that done before it snowed—it's gonna snow this weekend, you know."

"Mm-hm."

After a long moment, he added, "I think you're just circling around my house. Yeah, see? Turn down here and you'll pass Immaculate Conception."

I slowed the car to a halt at a stop sign kitty-corner to the school. "Why would Sandy go to your house?" I flashed my lights at the Prius waiting for me to move.

"Why not? I mean, I'm dead, right?"

"Yes, but as far as I'm aware, no one has contacted her about your death. She isn't listed as your next-of-kin, your brother is."

"Ah-hah. That makes sense. If the cops talked to Charlie, he or Mary probably called her to keep an eye on things till they drove down—they live in Ann Arbor up over in Michigan now. Even if they left immediately, it'd still take 'em at least four hours to get here."

What was the harm in reversing my search from outward-in to inward-out? One way or another, we'd eventually find Sandy, though I'd prefer sooner rather than later; the more time I had to work on convincing her to show me the sword, the better.

I tapped Teddy O'Byrne's address into the GPS on my phone and tracked the route on the map. Five-minute drive, the ETA at 5:12. Not bad. I turned right.

Teddy, however, proved himself to be perhaps the most appalling of backseat drivers I've ever had the unwanted privilege of carting around.

"Turn left!" Teddy's arm snapped up and out. Probably meant to put his pointing finger in front of my face but instead, managed to sink his whole incorporeal hand through my head. Sparklers went off behind my eyeballs and my lips went numb from the contact. I jerked the steering wheel to keep from dive-bombing a parked minivan. "Hey! You gotta turn left here—hey, you hear me? Turn—"

"Love of all *gods,* man, take your *hand* out of my *head*."

Teddy sat back with a grunt that wasn't actually an apology, but the tone was close enough. I flexed my jaw and smacked my lips to work the feeling back into my flesh. I braked at the next stop sign. Teddy refrained from gesturing again, though he squirmed like he wanted to.

"You should've turned there," he said.

"I know where I'm going."

"Yeah, but that was a shortcut."

"I am not driving down pothole-ridden alleys for a shortcut."

"It would've saved time." Teddy held up his hands as if to fend off my protestations. "I'm just sayin'."

I gritted my teeth and almost missed the correct turn just to spite him, but figured it wasn't worth the lecture about my directional sense, or apparent lack thereof.

♣

Teddy's house was a squat, one-story ranch with blue-gray siding, gray roof, and white trim around the windows and front door, with a pair of well-groomed evergreen bushes under the bay windows in front and a long driveway along the side that led into the backyard. The lights were off. The charmed vial around my neck hummed in time with the blood of another O'Byrne close by.

I pulled into the driveway.

Somewhere beyond, a dog barked.

"I think that's Benny," Teddy said, then promptly phased through the passenger-side door and took off down the driveway.

I threw the car into park and yanked out the keys, kicked my door open just in time to see Teddy disappear around the back of the house. With more caution than speed, I jogged down the driveway, past the white garage doors, and plastered myself to the wall to peek around the corner.

No sign of Teddy.

But there was a woman standing in the middle of the dying lawn that dominated the center of the backyard, holding a broadsword leveled at the Weber grill tucked against the seven-foot-tall picket fence dividing Teddy's property from his neighbor's. The porch light mounted over the back door bathed the yard in harsh, white light and deep, crisp-edged shadows, and the lawn was the pale green-and-straw of frost-dormant grass, receding from the edge of the concrete patio that hugged the back porch.

She wasn't how I'd pictured Sandy O'Byrne. Although, admittedly, my mental image was mostly stereotypical Hollywood badass in leather and long, straight hair. The Sandy O'Byrne of actuality had to be almost six feet of solid, fat-lined muscle and channeled both the strength and general body shape of a black bear. Her hair was cut short in tight curls and dyed a vibrant pink fading into magenta at the tips. Despite the almost thirty-five-degree weather, she wore a pair of yoga pants and a loose t-shirt, the bottom of which was tied in a makeshift bow at the base of her waist. Her arms were studded with tattoos and gleamed with a layer of sweat.

She turned—no, pivoted, for the motion had too much grace and control for a turn—and, in a flurry of movement, brought the broadsword up and around in what I guessed was a block or parry, then dropped low for a jab at the stomach of an invisible opponent. Sandy O'Byrne might be built like a bear, but she moved like a dancer. Her shadow on the fence jerked and spun.

I leaned a little farther out around the corner and caught sight of Teddy on his knees in front of a squat, round dog that looked a cross between a Black Labrador perched on a Bulldog's short legs. Teddy's hands phased through either side of the dog's neck and Benny leaped backwards as if shocked.

"Benny!" Teddy wailed, a mix between apology and something like loving reprimand.

Benny looked to the left, to the right, sneezed once, then whined.

"Benny?" Teddy's expression fell, a mix between heartbreak and dismay. *Damn,* I should've warned him. A ghost's touch could manifest as anything from a sense of extreme coldness right through to an electrical shock, and if you couldn't see the ghost in question—which went for pretty much everyone, excepting the magically inclined and certain spiritual sensitives—the experience was a baffling and unpleasant one. For a dog? The poor thing probably thought it was being zapped by air.

Benny sniffed at Teddy's general direction. Teddy went to reach again and grazed the dog's ear. The dog yelped and bolted for the other side of the yard on, albeit, short legs that gave it a distinct waddling gait.

Sandy O'Byrne paused in her workout. "Benny? What the hell—what are you doing now?" The dog sped past her and darted under a pair of balding evergreen bushes along the section of the fence facing the alley. "Hey! Out of Uncle Teddy's bushes! You know you're not supposed to go back there—oh, come on, dog…"

Definitely Cassandra O'Byrne, then.

So what the hell was I supposed to do now? Walk over and ask her to show me the sword? If the sword she was holding *was Fragarach.* I had my doubts; the ankou's tasks were rarely that easy. Though if the ankou was to be trusted, the sword could, potentially, not be a literal sword when sheathed. Which left the question, how was I supposed to get it to manifest?

Sandy smacked the flat side of the broadsword against the fence and Benny scuttled out from his hiding place.

Perhaps I was overcomplicating this. Perhaps it really was as straightforward as simply being polite.

I took a deep breath, held my hands up in semi-surrender, and stepped around the corner and out into Teddy's yard.

"Cassandra O'Byrne?" I called.

"Yeah? Who the fuck're you?"

"My name's Clay." *Come on, Clay, you don't have a better plan here.* "I was wondering if you knew anything about a sword called *Fragarach*?"

Which, apparently, was precisely the wrong thing to say. The tip of Sandy's broadsword came up in a motion that screamed *en garde!* and she sprang sideways along the fence, coming at me at a slight angle with the apparent intent to cut off my retreat down the driveway.

So much for being straightforward and polite.

I took a step back. Sandy waved with the sword in challenge, a silent *go ahead, fucker, I dare you.*

"Well, that wasn't very bright," Teddy said to my left and far, far too close, and I would've shot upward out of my very skin right then if I could. Gods *damn* but ghosts moved quietly when they didn't realize they should be making noise.

I stifled the squawk, did my best to turn it into a cough. Still, Sandy stared askance at me with a hostile mix of suspicion and worry. "What the fuck's your problem?"

I coughed again. "Nothing, nothing, just… um… don't usually have swords pointed at me, that's all. Makes me nervous." And winced at the sheer stupidity of my lie.

She raised an eyebrow in a perfect *uh-huh* expression and brandished the sword at me again. I shifted direction and let her herd me to the center of the lawn to stand in the hard light.

"Turn around."

I did so, hands still up and to the side.

"Who are you?"

"I told you already."

"Yeah. Right." She gestured at me with the sword and I stepped back a pace. "What do you know about the sword?"

"Frankly? Not all that much. It's a sword, it's mythical, it's magic, and you're somehow connected to it, though I'm not exactly sure how. Oh, and there's something about sheaths and manifestation. But, yeah, that's about it." I raised my eyebrows and my tone and, half in hope, half in jest, added, "Do I get any points for being truthful?"

She snorted.

"I'm gonna say that's a no," Teddy put in. I threw a scowl his way and tried to indicate with a bump of my eyebrows that he ought to go someplace else and mind his own business. I was handling this. Sort of. Well, poorly, but it'd be handled. In the end.

Teddy shook his head. "Fine, fine. Just tryin' to help."

"Would you go sit by your dog?" I hissed out of the corner of my mouth.

Teddy's shoulders slumped. "He won't let me get anywhere near him."

"Because you're *dead*. Stop trying to pet him, he'll be fine."

"Hey!" Sandy shouted, snapping my attention from Teddy back to her. "If you're gonna talk, talk loud enough for me to hear, yeah?"

"Of course, of course," I said, raising my voice to a normal speaking level. Out of the corner of my eye, I watched Teddy, in turn, move away from me to sit—or, rather, hover in a seated position—on the top step of the wooden porch as close to Benny as he dared without touching the dog. His hand came up to pet Benny's head, then fell back, and he folded his hands between his knees.

The dog didn't react. Which, all things considered, was probably a harsher reminder of Teddy's death than seeing his own corpse on an examination table.

I opened my mouth to say… what? Sorry? To impart my sympathies? It all just seemed so inadequate. I closed my mouth, shook my head, and looked up to find Sandy staring at me.

Which she'd apparently been doing for a while, long and hard, her lips pinched and nostrils flared like she'd just sniffed a gallon of milk and was trying to decide if it was sour or not. "I don't have time for this shit," she said and, abruptly, suddenly, and above all *quickly* moved, crossing the distance between us in the time it took me to process she was no longer where she'd been and that damn sword was coming up to take my head off my shoulders.

With a yelp, I stumbled back and, simultaneously, reached metaphysical fingers down, down, and down, deep into the heart-veins of the world, and heaved up great fistfuls of magic, poured it into the massive roots of the maple tree in the yard next door.

The roots erupted from the lawn, coiled up and around Sandy's pumping legs, around her waist, up her back, but still she kept coming, twisting her body forward in a lunge, still bringing the sword around to hack right through my neck.

Desperation added to the brunt force of power playing through my fingers, and with a strangled *nnnnyaaaaagh* noise, I wrenched up another handful of roots and wrapped them around Sandy's sword arm, pushing it back, pushing the sword away from me.

Her momentum ground to a slow, staggering halt and the edge of the blade kissed the spot over my right carotid. So close, so damn close—I heaved a gasping breath, then another, as the reality of just how *frickin'* close I'd come to dying slammed down on me, bent my shoulders, my spine. I didn't even have the presence of mind to step back.

Sandy bared her teeth in a not-really-a-smile. Her eyes flickered from decision to resolution and she tipped her hand slightly, oh so slightly, and the flat of the blade pressed against the underside of my jaw.

"Clay whatever-your-name-is, I hereby bind you," she intoned, and it *was* an intonation. I've done enough bindings in my time to recognize that special level of intent.

Ripples of force crawled up my legs, through my arms, tightening my muscles, my limbs, like liquid concrete had been poured through my blood vessels. Belatedly, I went to step away but too late, far too late. The binding had me tight in its grip.

But then, I also had Sandy. Which made us a very strange tableau, two people frozen in midstep, one holding a sword and tangled in roots, the other apparently paralyzed, standing in a backyard in the middle of Norwood under the watchful eyes of a dog and a ghost.

With a tweak of power, I snuffed the porch light over the door, plunging the yard into darkness, and blinked as my eyes adjusted to the soft glow of the city's light pollution.

"Who are you?" Sandy said, her voice sharp and barking.

"I *told* you. I'm Doctor Claymore Atwater."

"Doctor?"

"I'm a pathologist. Employed as a medical examiner at Resurrection Hospital." Which was more than I usually said for a general introduction.

"Why are you here? What do you want with me?"

"I meant it when I said I was looking for *Fragarach*. I've been given a task, see, by an ancient Breton death personification that likes to try and set me up for failure whenever it can." Hold up, I didn't mean to say that. Well, not *all* of that. "Though when I say *given* a task, it's more like being compelled, seeing that I'm currently under a geas in punishment for my transgressions against nature—" Wait, wait! "—for trying to bring my brother back to life when he abruptly died of a brain aneurysm—" What the hell was I doing? "—and a certain magic council thought it fitting to let the ankou choose the punishment, though tweaked it just slightly so it wouldn't be utterly impossible—" I wasn't supposed to say this! "I am compelled, obligated, whatever you wish to complete seven by seven by seven—or three hundred and forty-three—tasks the ankou sets me—" Any of this! "—with the soul of a recently deceased individual being held as collateral. If I complete the task to the ankou's satisfaction, the soul goes on its way. If I don't, the ankou takes it. Which is precisely what happened to the ghost of your Uncle Teddy, who's been following me around, by the way, and makes a lot of unhelpful commentary and is a terrible backseat driver—" Oh, no, no, no, this couldn't be happening, this wasn't right! "—and I have a little more than five hours, give or take, to locate *Fragarach* and convince it to manifest itself for the ankou or else Teddy's soul is forfeit—" I gasped a breath and croaked, "I'm a fucking magician, damn it! How the hell are you compelling me?" *Fragarach.* The Answerer. As in, the one under its power—literally—had to answer. Oh, hell. "Magic, mythic sword." Fuck. "Never mind, I've worked it out for myself."

Although, if that broadsword was *Fragarach,* I seriously should lower my expectations of magical, mythical swords. It was… well, to put it kindly, plain. And a little… manufactured in its standard-ness. But, I supposed, all the better for it to hide in plain sight.

Sandy did her best to lean the blade ever so slightly closer to my jugular. The cold edge grazed my skin. "What d'ya mean, you're talking to the ghost of my dead uncle?"

"Exactly that. He's over there." I jerked my thumb at the porch. "Next to Benny."

"You're telling the truth. Or you're crazy and you just *think* you're telling the truth."

I wiggled my fingers at the mass of roots holding her in place, the most movement I could accomplish while bound and compelled. "Magic, yeah?"

"Magic. Gotcha." She fell silent, her gaze focused on the ground. "Well, fuck." She looked up at me, her mouth set in a firm frown. Not disbelieving simply… disturbed. "So Uncle Ted's really a ghost?"

"Yup."

"And he's caught up in some kind of curse?"

"Yup."

She twitched her off-hand, held suspended in place by a root lashed around her wrist, in a half-hearted little wave. "Hey, um, hi, Uncle Teddy." Then muttered, "I cannot *believe* I just did that," just as Teddy called out, "Hi, Sandy."

"He says hi. And now he's waving."

Sandy shook her head. "This is so fucking bizarre."

*Story of my life.* Bizarre, weird, strange, often paired with the baffling, the wondrous, and the sometimes downright soul-wearying. Without really intending to, I sagged forward a little. The blade pressed against my throat, the edge digging into my skin, and I jerked back.

And, with a jolt, realized— "That sword isn't sharp!"

Sandy gave me a look that practically screamed *no, duh!* "Of course it isn't, it's a practice blade, you idiot."

"Oh." I mulled over the implications of that. "Oh, wait. If that's not *Fragarach* and you're still able to bind and compel me then… ah, *shit*, the sword's in you, isn't it? Or you are *Fragarach*… no, you're the sheath." If I hadn't been bound, I could've slammed my heel against the ground right then and done some pointless though expressive stalking around in circles. "Ah, hell. This is *exactly* what I didn't want, this is exactly what I wanted to avoid. This never ends well—"

"What d'ya mean, it never ends well?"

"—next time, I swear by any and all gods who care to bear witness—"

"Hey! You've seen something like this—me—before?"

"—if it asks me to find a human, I'll refuse. I'll refuse! No idea what'll happen then, but I'm done with this—"

"Clay! Claymore!" The tension in her arm relaxed slightly and the sword drooped, the flat of the blade resting on my shoulder. Sandy cocked her head at me. "Seriously, your name is actually 'Claymore'?"

"Says so on my driver's license." Sandy opened her mouth for the inevitable slew of questions and, stifling a sigh, I cut her off, "Yes, my name really is Claymore, I chose it for myself when I was sixteen and had all my identification changed to reflect it once I was legally able. It had and still has meaning to me, though I do sometimes wish sixteen-year-old-me had thought through the potential fallout of picking something so damn unusual. But, for simplicity's sake, I mostly go by Clay. Happy?"

"You know, it kinda does make me… relieved? that your parents didn't name you after a kind of sword."

"They didn't." Instead, my mother had named me Anne.

Which was far beside the point and while we still had a few hours before the ankou's deadline, now that I wasn't moving, the weather was starting to creep up on me. I suppressed another shiver. "Okay, look. How about we both back off, okay? You unbind me, I release the roots, and we have a nice, normal conversation?" Preferably indoors with central heat?

Sandy chewed on my offer, her gaze darting from me to the porch—not quite lighting on Teddy—then over to Benny and back again. She huffed. "Fine. I release thee, Claymore Atwater—I still can't believe that's your actual name—from this binding."

The hardened concrete in my veins shattered and I stumbled back, finishing that step I'd never been able to complete. Likewise, I coaxed the tree roots to unwind and bury themselves again in the earth, then released the stranglehold I had over the porch light, which flared to life.

"You ripped up my lawn, you know," Teddy said.

I flung my hands out to either side. "Look, *sorry,* but I thought your niece was trying to decapitate me." Then, noticing Sandy's expression, I relayed Teddy's comment out loud by way of explanation to avoid looking too much like a madman.

Sandy waved my words aside. "What did you mean, this kind of thing never ends well?"

I sighed and shoved my hands in my coat pockets. Without the threat of nearly dying or the rush of magical power, my fingers were really starting to freeze. Should've worn gloves but then, I didn't think

I'd be standing around outside this long. "Just that. Humans are hard and don't cooperate and I swear, the ankou is doing this on purpose. Trying to trip me up, make me fail, without actually violating the terms of the bargain. I think it's looking for a loophole." It came out rather more morose than I'd intended.

"So what? To save my uncle's soul, I have to let you kill me or something so you can take the sword?"

"What? No! I was just tasked to find *Fragarach* and make it manifest. The ankou doesn't want it, it just wanted to give me a task that would've been nearly impossible to complete if your uncle hadn't remembered you had that tattoo on your shoulder. Which… you know, come to think of it, I'm surprised the ankou didn't add a gag-order to the bargain. Letting Teddy talk might've been a mistake, unless it suspected you weren't going to cooperate and hoped we'd be at this till past the deadline."

"Or maybe this… ankou, whatever it is, hoped I'd stab you or something."

"Eeeeeh, probably not. It gets its kicks when I fail. If I'm dead—or hospitalized—it doesn't get to have its fun." Though I wouldn't put that past it, if it was getting frustrated with trying to think up tasks for me for every ghost I came across. Which were appallingly numerous, given that I worked at a morgue.

Sandy shifted her weight from side to side and, slowly, blew out a breath. Steaming coils of condensation streamed from her nose, the first sign that she was affected whatsoever by the temperature. If I'd been wearing that getup, I'd have been close to suffering the beginnings of hypothermia.

"So… all you need is just to see the sword?" she asked.

"Pretty much."

"And you—or this ankou—aren't going to try and take it?"

I grimaced. "I don't think we can. At least, I don't think *I* can, not without trying to kill you—"

"Fat chance."

"I did say *trying*, you know. And the ankou… is a supernatural being and death personification. I don't think it'd have a use for a sword, even if it could somehow separate it from you." I did my best to point at the broadsword through my coat pocket. "And if the sword is corporeal, I don't think it could pick it up. And if it's incorporeal, neither can I."

"And if I help you, it lets Uncle Teddy go?"

"Yup."

She nodded.

And swung the sword up and around, angling it edgewise so the blade bisected her face. Her eyes closed and she began to hum—tunelessly, yes, but not without rhythm. It sounded less like music and more like magic. I let my perceptions sink into the current weaving around her, let my awareness skim the edges of her working. Her heartbeat thumped through the back of my skull and I followed the trails of magic from her heart down out through her hand, into the sword, and back again.

To another magician, this level of scrutiny would've been rude. Kennett, were he still alive, would've smacked me across the side of the head for it and called me a pervert. But magic… magic was so damn intoxicating in its beauty, its vitality, and Sandy didn't seem to have any awareness whatsoever of my presence on the sidelines, same way she had no perception of her uncle's ghost.

And then the sword *changed.* Not physically—it was still the same blunt-edged practice broadsword made more for building up muscle mass in your arms than actually hacking and slashing. More… metaphysically. It gained another dimension, a different kind of weight, of solidity, of presence.

It became, for all intents and purposes, *Fragarach.*

Sandy lowered the sword.

"So," I said after a moment, "does it have to be a sword for that to work?"

She shrugged. "Not really. I mean, it's easier if it looks like a sword already, yeah, but I've done it with kitchen knives, broom handles, toy swords from the dollar store, tree branches, though I usually either go with one of my own swords or the crowbar in the back of my car. Did it with a plastic rake once, though I was pretty desperate when that happened."

I nodded in understanding. "Things that can evoke a sword's image." Things you'd see a kid pick up and wave around, saying it was Excalibur or what have you. Things that lent themselves as *sword* to the imagination, for the boundaries between imagination and magic, in the hands of a skilled practitioner, were easily permeable.

"Something like that, yeah. Doesn't really work for couch pillows."

My lip quirked in a smile.

"What now?" she asked.

"We wait for the ankou to show up. Shouldn't be long. It's got a pretty good sense about these—"

The roaring rush of a whirlwind I couldn't feel sped past me, stealing away my words in a flurry of wind and the flutter of owl wings, and from the sharp shadows spattered across the back fence, the ankou's shape coalesced.

Beside me and, a little faintly, Sandy said, "Okay, yeah, I can see that."

The ankou rolled its shoulders, cracked its neck, and stretched its jaw, as if reacquainting itself with this shape. "What do you bring me, child?"

"The task you set to me is done. I present to you—" I waved my hands at Sandy and the sword like a stage magician. "—*Fragarach*. Happy?"

The ankou tilted its head. "Hmmmm, rarely happy, child. Call it more *satiated*. Very well. I bear witness that you have completed this two hundred and sixteenth task. You have searched—and found—a shard of *Fragarach*. And so completes the bargain. You!" The ankou's voice barked out like the crack of a whip and it pointed at Teddy behind me. "And so you are freed from this one's curse, the tethers around your soul are loosed. Get thee gone to wherever fate will have you," the ankou intoned, then flipped its hand in a dismissive gesture at poor Teddy.

"But—wait—that's it? That's all?" Teddy barely managed to rise before his edges started breaking apart and dissipating again, his form and presence blurring, bits of the blue-gray siding of the house and scraps of the porch steps showing through his torso in flickers and snatches. He smacked his incorporeal hands against his torso as if trying to put his disintegrating body back together. Or, at least, hold back the disintegration for as long as he could.

"But I'm not ready!" he cried. I resisted the urge to look away. Gods, this was never easy. Some ghosts go in peace, others rage against the unfairness of it all. Teddy, it seemed, was going to be a rager.

The ankou clicked its tongue, shook its head, and, with the wailing of a train whistle, its edges *crack*-snapped out of sync with the corporeal world. The echoing rattle of wheels on a track and the rustle of cloth snapping in the breeze faded.

I turned to Teddy. Teddy held his fragmenting hands out to me.

"You can still see me, right? Right? I need you to ask Sandy, please, take care of Benny for me, okay? Take care of Benny!"

I passed the message along. Sandy's expression crumpled in grief and shock. "God, of course, of course I will, I couldn't—I mean, Christ, of *course*. But—oh, *shit*, I don't think my apartment lets in pets!"

"That doesn't matter! Tell her she can have my house! 'S better for Benny anyway, not having to move from his home, and it's not like I got any kids to leave it to. It's willed to Charlie—her dad. Just—tell her to tell Charlie that I wanted her to have the house but didn't get a chance to change my will. And tell her you're going to fix my goddamned lawn!"

I ignored that last though I probably would pay to have the lawn fixed; my brand of magic didn't lend itself to neat landscaping. "I hate to be a pessimist here, but will he believe that?" I said to the quickly-dissipating shreds of Teddy's ghost.

"If he doesn't, tell him I'm coming back to haunt his ass! Like in that movie—" But his voice was already fading, and his form was down to a flicker of a face and his outstretched left hand. And then, he was gone.

"Take care of my dog," the last echo of his voice whispered in my ear. "Take care of my dog."

I swallowed down the lump lodged in my throat. Coughed to clear away the last vestiges of the obstruction.

Quietly, I said, "He's gone."

"Yeah." Sandy's shoulders bunched up around her ears and she looked away from me, the harsh light putting her face in shadow, hiding her expression. "Yeah, I figured."

She whistled once, short and sharp. Benny's ears perked up and she clicked her tongue against her teeth, gesturing at the back door. Benny bounced to his feet and thumped up the stairs to the porch and, slower, Sandy followed. Then stopped, one foot on the bottom stair, and looked back at me. She clicked her tongue again. Exasperation or resignation, I couldn't quite tell.

"You want a cup of coffee or something?"

"That'd be very kind, thank you," I said, and followed her and Benny up the stairs and into what had been Teddy O'Byrne's home.

Sometimes, there's something to be said for straightforward quests.

# THE LADY OF THE LAKE

## *P. J. RICHARDS*

Moonlight splintered across the surface of the Lake in Central Park.

The woman threw something into its silvered expanse, reaching her arm back to heft the weight, bending forward with the follow-through. It looked like a long blade but he couldn't be sure; the ambient light was dimmed by a rising mist, and she was silhouetted against the broken reflection of streetlamps and the Midtown skyline. A splash leapt from the Lake as it hit, but by the time the ripples reached the shore she was gone.

Nearby sirens whooped above the rumble of traffic then died away. A cackle of laughter, shrill and manic, drifted from the edges of the Park. There was no way of telling if it was human or Unseelie, but it wasn't worth the risk in finding out. He turned his back on the quiet water and retraced his steps, careful to keep to the path.

In the shadows between lamp posts, fireflies scrawled indecipherable runes in the air, and will-o'-the-wisps drifted, enticing a careless step. He touched the torc of thin twisted iron around his neck, and quickened his pace.

A low mound of solid rock loomed ahead, curved and smooth. It was crowned with a boulder, and the ghost of the glacier that had carried then dropped it there, flowed over the outcrop as a faint shimmering aura. He checked around to make sure he was alone, before scrambling up its side – knowing he risked attracting attention by his speed, but calculating that it would buy him enough time to find the woman's mark before the banshees sensed he'd left the path.

At the summit, the long-lost light blended with the glow from the moon, wrapped him and chilled him, tasting of ice, grit and endless winter. He pulled back from its bitter embrace, and focussed on the ordinary lights cast by the nearby lamps and buildings, borrowing their blandness to stay unnoticed. Under his feet lay a parchment of stone, polished by millennia of grinding ice cliffs. And there, carved into the hard, grey schist, shone a fresh cup-and-ring mark.

The straight line was long, indicating the effort of the throw he'd just witnessed. He crouched to examine the neat circle at its end depicting the hit, which was gouged deep enough to take his thumb, and then brushed his fingers over the seven concentric rings of ripples scored around it. A substantial gift. His eyes hadn't tricked him, it must indeed have been a sword.

The latest carving lay nestled beside the previous eleven, and their depiction of the woman's work gave life to the stone, transforming its static surface to water dimpled with swirling motion. The etched lines portrayed long throws and short, small splashes and large, reviving a forgotten prehistoric ritual to create a permanent record of a profound, but ephemeral, act of sacrifice. In the Old World, cup-and-ring marks remained a mystery – here in the New, the woman had engraved their truth for him to find.

He checked the surrounding trees for eyes, saw none and took out his phone, ready to take a photograph of her latest petroglyph.

A scream ripped through the park, brought him staggering to his feet. He spun around trying to locate the sound as it tailed off into a desolate whine. It tore the air again in a frenzied, falling shriek: sucking the air from his lungs, burning his limbs with adrenalin, crushing his mind beneath blank animal terror. The stench of rot replaced the sweetness of dirt and leaves and fumes on the warm night air.

He ran for his life.

♣

The next morning, he went back to the Park.

Sunshine steadied his nerves, daylight rendered the landscape friendly again. Joggers overtook him, tourists took selfies, kids fed the ducks, suits talked too loudly on their cells. The power of the mundane ruled.

He bought a coffee and walked to Bow bridge, stepping on the flowers of light cast onto the pale boards through the cinq-foil pattern in the railings. Wooden rowboats trailed wakes of laughter and ripples from clumsily slapped oars. The circles of disturbed water summoned up an image of the woman by the Lake: always with her back to him, outlined by the city's geometric indifference, cradling and then casting away something precious. Her dark hair fanning like a cape over her shoulders, her long dress trailing in the shallows. How she sometimes hesitated for a heartbeat or two after the waters swallowed her offerings, before running into the shadows.

The thought of her stung him with a confusion of anxiety and desire. He fingered the iron torc, squeezing the spiral finials tighter to his throat. The more he tried to convince himself that she was completely human the more he became aware of her uncanny ways; how she could carve the rock and be gone before he reached it, her ability to pass unnoticed by the hunt. And yet there was something deeply familiar about her, a kinship that he never felt from the other denizens of the Park at night. From those beautiful, terrifying settlers who had made this contrived wilderness their home, and those fellow enraptured mortals who ventured in, risking death - or worse - for a chance to experience true magic.

The banshee screams from the night before still echoed in his head, and the police-tape strung like a fluorescent web across the stone steps down to Ramble Cave, indicated that there would be one less wanderer out tonight. The Unseelie hunters had found their prey, and the sense of relief that it hadn't been him was selfish and ruthless, a primitive glee. He felt no sympathy for the victim.

Everyone knew that you shouldn't go into Central Park after dark.

♣

When night fell he was ready to go back in. This time he was determined to see her face. A resolution born of the need to prove she was human. One look at her eyes would be enough. Then, if she was Unseelie after all, he could stop wasting his time searching for her, and instead go back to exploring the other realms of the Park—be himself and forget her. Return to spending hours listening to the singers in the trees; watching shining Lir swans, wings fluting with each beat, glide down to scatter ducks like blown leaves; follow the Seelie Court's golden processions through the woods at the turning of the seasons; run wild along the trails, kicking up cascades of cold green sparks; dodging flint arrows and vicious needle-teeth and dagger-claws. Racing the blissful danger like he used to.

Stop giving in to the compulsion to follow her, or hear her speak. Or see her smile. Or feel her touch. Or lose himself within her.

He walked to the rock outcrop. It loomed above him, haloed in the light of its past. It was the sole form of communication he had with the woman, but it was a one-sided dialogue; he only ever glimpsed her leaving. Three times he had skipped the gift giving at the Lake to wait for her here, in the hope of catching her arrival. She never showed up, yet he would inevitably find a new cup-and-ring mark the next time he checked.

This time he was going to put his faith in the magic of technology.

He strapped a motion-sensor camera to the closest tree. If she climbed the rock this time her image would be captured, and even if her back was to the lens it would reveal her nature. No picture he'd ever taken of the Seelie or Unseelie had ever shown anything more than vague shapes and shadows or unfocussed glowing orbs.

He prayed that the screen would show her face. If it was just a haze, and proved that an enchantment had been slipped into his heart, he would suffer. He had come across the consequences of such infatuations before: most pined to death in the Park, unable to eat or sleep, mistaken for junkies, curled up and cold on benches. But some ends were less gentle. One night he found a woman lying face down inside a ring of toadstools, blood from her torn throat being sucked up greedily by a swarm of dragonfly-winged Unseelies, and the sweet laughter of what she had loved - and doubtless believed had loved her back - fading as a fox-tailed girl in a dripping red gown danced carelessly away.

After checking twice that the camera was set up correctly, and then once more for luck, he set off for the Lake.

The woman was waiting.

She was standing in the shallows, ankles lapped with tiny silver waves, holding her hands cupped before her as if around a precious book. Abruptly, the serenity of the image was broken, as strands of her hair were snatched up and twisted by invisible fingers. She shook her head and swatted the teasers away, and it was such an ordinary human reaction that he was heartened. But then she raised her arms, holding her sacrifice, and her slender form was silhouetted against the obsidian mirror of the water and the gemstone constellations of the city, and the moon seemed drawn down to her, and all the traffic noise and the whirring night fell silent.

Light glinted off the edges of what she held. It was his camera.

She launched it high and hard, the lines of her body rigid with anger. In shock and dread, he stared at the curve of its flight, then at the hollow cup, and the spreading rings, marking where it vanished beneath the waters of the Lake.

And this time, when he looked back, she was still there.

# FAITH, BEGORRAH, AND OY GEVALTE!

*Art Lasky*

In the spring of 1952, back in Brooklyn, many homes and businesses were still heated by coal. Why is that important? Well, it sets the stage for what happened to young Sidney O'Grady in late March of that year; he fell down a coal chute. One minute 18-month-old Sidney was proudly walking along, not even holding mommy's hand, the next:

"Holy moly macarolly! I've fallen down a coal chute."

"No shit, Sherlock. I'm glad I was here to break your fall," said a muffled, but nonetheless sarcastic, voice coming from beneath him.

"Wait a minute, I'm talking, really talking, until now the best I've ever managed was: *more milkie, pease.*"

"Well, whoop de doo for you. Are ya gonna get offa me or what?" said the voice.

"Oops, sorry pal. I didn't look where I was going and WHOOSH right down the chute."

"I noticed. Now get the heck offa me ya bastid!"

Sidney immediately scrambled to his feet, surprising himself, with the agility of a three-year-old. Scampering off the mound of coal, he looked back and saw a little man, no bigger than a two-year-old. The man's clothes, which he was dusting off and straightening after having been an involuntary pillow, were all green. He wore a, slightly crushed, derby and a pipe was clenched firmly in his mouth. His hair and fringe of a beard were red.

"What are you?" the boy asked.

He shot Sidney an icy look, muttering something about kids and manners,

"I'm a Leprecohen, ya ignoramus."

"You mean Leprechaun."

"So, you're an expert on the wee folk, are you? I said Leprecohen, I meant Leprecohen!"

"You don't even sound Irish," said Sidney.

I'm third generation away from home, but my great-grandad was from Donebagel, a wee village two day's donkey east of Galway."

"'Never heard of the place," young master O'Grady replied. "I'm from Flatbush, myself… So what's the difference between Cohens and Chauns?"

"Well, we Cohens don't work on Saturday. And instead of a pot of gold, we put a pot of diamonds at the end of our rainbows."

"Wow, diamonds!" Sidney was immediately intrigued and scanned the basement for a rainbow to follow.

"Don't get too excited, they're mostly SI1, poor color and the biggest is maybe half a carat."

"Still that's nothing to sneeze at," said the boy.

From way up above at the top of the chute, he could hear his mom making a scene.

"Oh my god! Someone help! My baby fell down the coal chute, help, help, HELP!"

It was hard to carry on a decent conversation with the racket, so he shouted up to her.

"Would you quiet down Mom, don't get your bloomers in a knot, I'll be right up."

For some reason that only got her screaming louder—go figure.

"So what are you doing down here, sitting on a pile of coal?"

The Leprecohen held up a pot, "waiting for this coal to turn into diamonds, what else?"

"Doesn't that takes thousands of years?"

The Leprecohen shrugged. "Ich bin en kyna gansa kamish." (I'm in no big rush.)

Suddenly Sidney, knew Yiddish too—oy!

At this point, the screaming and crying from the street was becoming way too intrusive.

"Look, pal, great conversation, but between the noise up above, and my over-ripe diaper down below, I better leave," said Sidney.

"So, am I stopping you? Go, already. Take the first door on the left, it's one flight up to the street."

"Thanks, buddy."

The further he got from the Leprecohen's magic the less coordinated he became. Turns out it was the wee-folk magic that allowed the boy to walk and talk so well.

Sidney toddled back to his mother as fast as his 18-month-old legs could go. He couldn't wait to tell her about his fabulous adventure. Unfortunately, sans magic, "More milkie, pease," was the closest he could come to a meaningful explanation.

# CAVE CANEM

*Ed Ahern*

Originally Published in *Liquid Imagination*, 2015

Phil's GPS went blank four miles from the house. After back-tracking twice on two-rut trails he finally was able to follow the sound of a generator into an overgrown parking area. The log house squatted under old-growth swamp oaks, house and trees tinged green with fungus.

How bad, he wondered, do I really need this job? Bad enough. He got out of the car and skirted alder and birch saplings to get to the front door.

Cernunos answered Phil's second round of knocking.

"You're Phil."

Phil doubted anyone else would trek out to this dump. He looked up six inches into Cernunos' mottled face and thought of a gravel bed.

"Mr. Cernunos, thank you for considering me…"

"Your uncle recommended you. You do remember the crazy old bastard that most people in your family couldn't stand?"

"Ah, yes."

"Okay. I'm older and nastier than he was. Not as randy maybe. Don't bother sucking up to me, you can hold onto the aurochs crap for people who need fertilizing. Something to drink?"

"Yes, sir. What do you have?"

"Barrel water or honey liquor. The mead's homemade. It's got an aftertaste of forest floor, but better than the industrial grade alcohol they'll sell you in town."

"I've never had mead. How's it made?"

"A sextarius of rainwater kept in oak barrels for three years, blended with a libra of honey and allowed to ferment."

"Um, maybe I'll just have water."

"Okay, it's from the same rain barrel."

They scooped their drinks from barrels inside the crudely finished cabin. The interior temperature and humidity were both about 90. Phil dropped sweat. Cernunos wafted a farm-like body odor. They went outside with their drinks to take advantage of a breeze. As they sat on a pair of tree stumps Phil noticed a large pile of antlers, bigger than eastern deer horns- elk maybe, but there were no elk around here.

"Do you collect those antlers Mr. Cernunos?"

"Sort of. They get shed once a year, and once a year I throw another pair of antlers on the pile. It's like a calendar for me."

Phil gathered that the old man was about as spin drifty as his uncle had been. "Mr. Cernunos..."

"Call me Cernunos, no mister. It's not my real name anyway, just a name some Romans gave me."

Crazy, Phil thought, definitely crazy. I wonder if he can pay me? "Oh. Anyway, I appreciate your considering me for this position. Not everyone would consider hiring an ex-convict."

"I investigated you. You're a convicted felon. That makes you desperate for work, which you'd have to be to take this job. As crimes go I'm partial to yours. You caught your wife in bed with a friend and beat him so badly that he's still crippled. But you didn't hit your wife. Means you still loved her. Rage and passion. I'm comfortable with that. Noble emotions. Not like today, just spite and greed."

"Greed?"

"Taranis' thunder rumble! Look. You're apt to be killed on the whim of a storm, but still assume you're entitled to riches, good looks, and a wonderful life. Don't get me started.

"And you're not hired yet, sonny. First we'll see if you can break loose from the civilized cocoon silk you're wrapped up in."

"Sir?"

"Here's the deal. You get a month to demonstrate your worth. I'll pay you by the week- two thousand dollars cash per week, no records.

You live here, you work here, you do everything I tell you to. Everything. You fail a test you leave. You can't deal with how I live, you leave. I don't like you because you stutter, you leave."

"I'm can't do anything illegal."

"I won't ask you to do anything you'll be prosecuted for. There's no television here, no radio, no cell phone signal. The electricity is for the computer and the bootleg phone line, which you can't use."

Phil hesitated. "Is there indoor plumbing?"

"Of course not. But there's a squatter out back.

"How do you shower?"

"It rains pretty often, and there's a brook with a plunge pool. I don't recommend the pond unless you move fast- the leeches and all. Oh, and no ice box."

"What do you eat?"

"Fresh and hung game, roots, wild apples and blueberries. I do have a weakness for Sugar Pops and canned milk for breakfast, but the cereal has gotten moldy. Doesn't bother me but you may not like it."

"A month?"

"A month. I pay you every week, so you can walk on a Friday with money in hand."

"Where will I stay on the weekends?"

"Esus' gnarly oak! You don't leave here for a month unless I take you somewhere."

"Mr. Cernunos, not to pry, but what can I do for you out here that's still legal and worth this kind of money?"

"If you last the month you'll know."

Phil was a beggar with little choosing available. They shook hands. Cernunos' hand was rough, almost barky. Phil got an advance of $300 for a last night in town and the purchase of toiletries and food he couldn't live without.

He was back at the cottage at daybreak. Cernunos was waiting. He handed Phil a stone bladed knife, the handle wrapped in strips of deerskin. It was wickedly sharp.

"You have four days to make a knife like this. The stone is chert. Obsidian gives a better edge and chips easier, but I'm old-fashioned. I've gathered some rough stones for you to work with. Three of them. If you break all three without producing a workable knife you leave."

"But I've never made a knife. I don't know how to start."

"That's what these other stones are for. Use them to chip out a double-edged blade. One tip- the smaller the pieces you chip off the better the knife, but the slower the work. I won't answer any more questions until you're done or gone."

"But I don't know where to sleep—"

"Gather some young branches and lay them out in a corner of the house. Fir works best."

Phil grabbed up the stones and walked back to the stump he had been sitting on the day before. He knelt in front of the waist-high stump and picked up a shaping stone, rounded at one end, pointed at the other. It fit his hand surprisingly well.

He worked through the day, pausing only to eat some of the food he had brought. Just before sunset the first stone snapped in two.

The next morning Phil rose with the shading of false dawn. His back and shoulders ached from the distortions of sleeping on branches. His hands, chafed and raw, stung as sweat touched them. He knelt again and studied the second stone for its seams and flaws.

The money, he reminded himself, just think about the money. The swelling and stiffness in his hands eased as he worked. His left hand, holding the unfinished knife blade, began to bleed onto the stone from stray cuts. Phil discovered that if he rubbed the blood into the chert he was better able to see the grain of the stone. By the end of the day he had deliberately cut himself twice to get more blood. And he finished chipping out the stone, blade and handle. It was deformed and ugly compared with Cernunos' blade, but it would cut.

The third morning Phil cut a strip of hide from an over-aged hanging deer and wrapped the haft. The skin was uncured and smelled of meat rot, but like the knife itself was serviceable. He took it to Cernunos.

"Well, Bridget's pointy tits, you've actually made something like a knife. You've fed it with your blood, which is good. Will it cut?"

"I think so."

That night Cernunos had Phil drive him for three hours into the nearest city. They wound through several streets before reaching the closest thing the town had to a barrio. It was almost 10 p.m. and the streets were owned by swaggering young men.

"Bring your knife with you," Cernunos instructed.

As they left the car and approached a run-down house Phil could hear fragments of Spanish spreading from boy to boy- "brujo," "pelegroso," as the young men faded backward.

At the door Cernunos was met by a wizened, dark-skinned man whose pronounced wrinkles looked like double folds.

"Quizachatel, are you still bedding down widows?"

"Are you still rutting with does?"

The two men smiled and embraced. They started speaking a foreign language, not Spanish, nothing Phil recognized.

"Come," said Cernunos, and they walked around the house to a chicken coop in the backyard. Inside the coop were several hens and a rooster. "Pick one," Cernunos instructed.

"What?"

"Pick out one bird. Take care which one you choose."

"What am I looking for?"

"Oh, Epona's hairy ass! Use your instinct. Before Lugos carts in the sun please."

Phil stared into the cage. One bird stared back. "Okay, that one, with the reddish speckles."

The wrinkled man stooped into the coop and grabbed the chicken. He walked over to a large block of wood and held the chicken down on it.

"Take out your knife and cut off the chicken's head."

"What!"

"Do it so the chicken head hangs over the edge of the block, otherwise your clothes are going to get sticky."

Phil argued, but lost. His knife blade hesitated at the feathers, but with pressure he was able to saw through the neck. More blood than Phil thought possible spurted down the side of the block.

The old man let go the dead chicken's body and backed away.

"Carefully cut open the bird's stomach and chest."

"Why?"

"You couldn't understand the answer. Just be careful not to damage the organs."

Phil gently inserted his knife and slit the skin upward toward the topless neck.

The old swarthy man pushed Phil aside, broke open the rib cage, and lowered his face into the entrails. After poking and sniffing he and Cernunos exchanged more unknown words.

"Succellos seems to be with you. Your omens are good."

"What's that mean?"

"You're not fired yet. Disembowel the chicken and wrap it in those rags. We're taking it with us."

"Why?"

"Because, cretin, we bought the chicken. We're going to take it home and eat it."

The next evening, after fire roasted chicken and mead, Cernunos leaned toward Phil. "What do you know about your uncle?"

"Not much. He was a loner, short-tempered and nasty. Most often gone somewhere. But he always had money, and when people in the family needed it he helped out, so he was tolerated."

"By Teutates, he was a real junkyard dog. Perfect. He worked for me for fifteen seasons, until his arthritis seized him up. His recommendation is why you're here."

"I'm not like him."

"Says the convicted felon. We'll find out."

Cernunos heard something inaudible to Phil and in a seamless movement was into the undergrowth. He was massive enough to still be visible in the twilight. Around him was blurred movement and snarling, some kind of animals.

Holy shit, Phil thought, what am I into. What is this thing I'm with?

Cernunos paced back into the yard.

"We have unwanted company."

"Huh?"

"Some of your criminal associates. They've started up a meth cookery. I don't want the attention that will bring. We're going to encourage them to leave."

"How?"

"You need to speak whole sentences, you'll sound more intelligent. You're going to kill one of them while they're sleeping."

"No I'm not, I'll get arrested."

"No, you won't. They can't report where they are or what they're doing. Oh, they might come back to try and kill us, but I'll handle that."

"Then you handle the first one."

"The first one is for the guard dog—that's you if you train up. If you can't do it I'll pay you through Friday and you can leave."

Phil started pacing. "He didn't do anything to me."

"Not relevant. They're trespassing, and your job is to make sure they don't come back. Can you handle it?"

"I can't kill him. I could maybe dust him up a little."

"Your cocoon is showing. Alright, just maim him."

"How bad would I have to hurt him?"

"Breaking both legs should be sufficient."

"What about the others?"

"I'll make sure they don't interfere."

Phil knew he needed at least another ten thousand dollars to get out from under. What the hell, he thought, these guys are trespassers, cooking up crystal meth. "All right."

Phil was awakened shortly after midnight and lead on an unlit trek through deep woods. Cernunos weaved through the undergrowth without hesitation. Phil again noticed how big Cernunos was, not fat, but maybe 300 pounds worth of massive. A little after 3 a.m. they approached a small clearing with a smoldering fire. Cernunos handed Phil a short-handled axe, not iron, bronze maybe, one side hammer-shaped the other side bladed.

"Your choice which side you hit him with." He pointed. "There—take the snoring one on the far side of the fire. He's the leader."

Phil edged around the clearing until he was next to the snoring man. Don't hesitate, he thought, the guy who gets in the first blow usually wins. His hands snaked out, one cupping the man's mouth, the other swinging the flat side of the axe into the man's left knee, shattering it. As the man lurched Phil leaned forward, chop stroking the hammer-head and breaking the left shin.

He jumped back into the thicket where Cernunos was waiting to lead him away. Behind them were yells and screams and a few random shots.

"You didn't tell me they had guns!"

"Quit whining. You weren't Ogmios, but I think you did manage to break his legs."

"Who the hell is Ogmios?"

"Think Hercules and you'd be close. While they're running around screaming we'll set fire to their lab."

It was an hour after dawn by the time they returned to Cernunos' cabin. Phil was drained, trembling from exhaustion and shock.

"I can't do that again."

"Stag droppings. You have the hunting temperament, you're just buried alive in social cloy. Living free means treading an edge so thin that there's a good chance you'll fall off and die. But it's worth it."

Phil studied Cernunos' mass. "I looked up your name, you know."

"Oh?"

"Google could only come up with some vagueness about a Celtic hunting god with horns. I assume you use the name as an alias?"

"Ah. Well. Something like that. Let's get some sleep."

The next week was devoted to ceremonies for which Phil had to memorize phrases- phrases whose knotty sounds forced him to move his lips and tongue in contorted ways.

"What's the purpose in all this? Why am I still killing animals?"

Cernunos lost patience. "Because I instructed you to—your understanding isn't necessary! Dis Peter, what I must do to survive! Can't you see that the world exists on blood sacrifice of one sort or another? You can't be a Vegan and practice real magic."

Cernunos had hunted deer that morning, and they dined that evening on fresh venison. As they tossed gristle and bone into the fire Cernunos glanced over at Phil.

"Our meth chefs are searching for us. They're braver than I credited."

"Where are they?"

"Searching the woods about a thousand passus away. I'll arrange that they don't discover the cabin."

"How? They've got guns."

"Yes, I suppose they do. Stay close to the cabin. Once I begin to hunt you all look alike to me."

Cernunos paced soundlessly into the woods, empty-handed.

Phil remained perched on his tree stump. Black clouded night seeped over the dusk. He strained, but heard nothing but insect noises. And then a yell. And more yells, and shots. And a scream. And then screams that were fainter and fainter until they stopped.

When Cernunos reentered the yard there were dark stains on his leather pants and shirt. He was still heaving in air, his nostrils flaring like an animal's.

"What sport I've had! The last was a runner, and I harried him for almost 500 passus before taking him down."

The fear hardened in him as Phil stared at the massive silhouette snorting in air and giving off musk. Whatever he is, Phil thought, he's not human. But he hasn't hurt me, and I really need the money. I can stick it out until after the fourth week.

"You stink of fear, little man. You're not some vestal virgin about to be raped. You're only a guard dog under training."

"What are you?"

"Ah. Much older than you think. More ominous than you yet believe. Use what you read about Cernunos. Get some sleep, heel hound, your training continues today."

The next two weeks were devoted to woods craft, mead brewing, and hunting and tracking. Phil's body fat shrank as his tendons and muscles defined. The wooded silence made small animal noises more apparent. Phil surprised himself with the enjoyment he took in tracking and killing game.

He noticed that Cernunos was growing two bumps on the sides of his forehead, covered in mossy velvet, but said nothing about them. On the fourth Friday Cernunos called Phil over and paid him the last $2,000.

"As dogs go you're still a cur, but you answer well to commands. I can use you for the next several months while I go into retreat. Same pay. Maybe a few more benefits. What your uncle did. Will you do it?"

Phil was unused to having a choice and paused. "Why are you going into retreat?"

"Because, mongrel, my horns are growing for the fall rut, and antlers will get me confined to a sideshow. I can cope here without you, but it's easier for me if you help out."

Phil's fear softened. "You need me now?"

"Yes you effete lap dog, I need you."

Phil savored the moment. "I want a real bed."

"You can have a cot."

"I want $3,000 a week."

"Very well."

"I want weekends off."

"May Belenos char you with his rays! Take care not to over gorge yourself, dog. You may have all weekends except the fall equinox."

"Okay, I'll do it. But…"

Cernunos didn't move but somehow loomed over Phil. "Be very careful, human."

Phil flinched but continued. "No, no, please—I only want you to keep teaching me while I'm here."

# THE ACHE OF WATER

*E.K. Reisinger*

Anders Doherty hovers over the saucepan of water and thinks of murder.

Outside, he hears the soft drone of cars, of erratic honks echoing off steel buildings, of metropolitan life moving. The smell of exhaust, of sewage and city, floats through Anders' open windows. Sam always thought Anders crazy for enjoying the stifling humidity of Houston, Texas.

A whirr of police sirens cuts over the city noise. Two, no three, cop cars in succession, speeding down the street in pursuit of some alleged crime. Closing his eyes, Anders sends a silent prayer to the mischief makers, whoever they may be. *Run*, he says. *Run. They are coming.*

His two brothers should have known Bridget was coming. Anders palms his back pocket, to his phone, where he got the call just two hours ago. His brother Sam was dead. Murdered, just like his other brother Leif, twenty years apart, by that fiery priestess Bridget. Anders grips the side of the counter, his red-rimmed sky blue eyes finding the window. Bridget left Anders with no family, no one, just a dingy city, an empty Houston apartment and a head full of dark thoughts.

Dark thoughts. Anders sets his jaw as an ache spreads in his chest. His blond head arches to the ceiling as tears fill his eyes. Anders always thought his magical lineage was more of a curse than a blessing. And now he knows it to be true. This mythical ancestry was a horrid hex.

*Run,* Anders would have said to his brothers, had he the gift of spirit, of seeing beyond linear time, beyond this world. *Run. She is coming.* Sniffling, he swallows, grips his blond hair in his hands. *Don't leave me.*

But they are gone. And he didn't have the spirit gift. Or fire, as Bridget did.

Anders' fingers crawl to his chest, to the large silver amulet hanging around his neck, safely tucked under his gray t-shirt. It is the sacred crest of The Thirteen, engraved with thirteen ogham symbols. Thirteen sacred, powerful Celtic families hidden for centuries. Forged in stolen Roman silver nearly two thousand years ago as his druid ancestors disappeared, the ancient amulet is the only atlas to his secret past. A lineage he and Bridget shared. A mystery he and his brothers were unraveling. Until now.

He wondered how his divine brethren would handle murder.

The blare of a horn jolts Anders back to the stove, the pan of water. With a flick of his hand, the water bubbles, instantly boiling. There were some benefits to who he was, he snorts. At least tea, swimming and pasta were never difficult.

*Eat.* Sam would have said, like a second father. *Everything is easier on a full stomach.* Dinner assembled, Anders pours himself a glass of merlot.

Outside, the sharp screech of a truck's brakes pierces the traffic hum. The crunching crash of metal colliding startles Anders. His arm flinches and his plate of fettuccine Alfredo upends, spreading across the table and spilling the wine. Cursing, Anders stumbles to the window. A three-car pile-up, one hood smoking, a truck jackknifed, a third car smashed in-between. Bystanders gather quickly, phones in hand, pulling staggering passengers to the curb. Anders looks back to the table, drops of blood red dripping from the side, a sea of creamy white and muted burgundy pooling on the top.

"Fuck," Tense hands to the ceiling, Anders shouts at the air. "FUCK!" Anger seizes him and he lurches to the table, turning it over in an easy shove. Wood and glass slide to the floor. He kicks a piece of plate with his foot, sending the stoneware sailing into the kitchen.

Shallow, rapid breaths take over his chest, his fingers grip his thighs. He allows the rage to come. Anders feels his coil of mysterious power deep inside, lets it pulse and grow. Muscles relaxing, his focus descends within, to his watery core, to where his enchanted gift, his druid curse, calls to the world. The first raindrops release from the sky, the tingling shooting from Anders like a climax, quick and hot. Moaning out a thick, long exhale, he lets the tidal wave of sensation hit him as it always does, in a heady, rushing flood. There will be no mercy today.

Deliberate and furious, he opens the door, strides down the hall, the stairs, to the building's door. He feels the water in his bones, in his entire being, but he needed to feel it on his skin. And his downpour today is magnificent.

A classic flash flood, the meteorologists would say. That strange, torrential rain that occasionally plagues Houston. Or, as Sam once said, the need for Anders to find a good therapist and leave Houston out of it.

The streets empty of people as the water pours from the sky. In mere minutes, rainwater pools in the sidewalk dips, the cradle of the curb, the overwhelmed drainage grates. The remains of the accident bear witness to Anders' wrath.

Today, he needed to let go. That quote from Genesis, from his Bible-quoting neighbor, rang in his ears. "For behold, I will bring a flood of waters upon the earth to destroy all flesh in which is the breath of life under heaven. Everything that is on the earth shall die."

Anders winces. *Don't play God Anders*, Sam would have said. *Use your sacred gift wisely.*

Water to his ankles now, Anders closes his eyes. The smell of rain, of wet cement folds around him. All he can hear is water. He stands among the muck of the streets, the debris of modernity, now submerged in a flood of his despair. Heavy rain pelts his upturned, smiling face as a guttural laugh escapes from his body.

*Run*, Anders hears himself say. *Run. I am coming.* Wrapping his fingers around the ancient amulet on his chest, Anders thinks of murder.

# GLANDOMIRUM

*Jarret Keene*

It rained in Las Vegas that night, a torrent that slicked the asphalt and neon and disoriented weed-vaping rideshare drivers, snarling Strip traffic and resulting in mournful horn honks and a few scary moments when an impatient local—some late-for-work employee speeding to a hotel-casino—would suddenly switch lanes, causing another vehicle to hydroplane. Airmid wasn't bothered by the delay, though. She'd just finished her set at Cleopatra's Barge for a rowdy group of tech conventioneers. They had joined her onstage for the rousing finale, a slightly alcoholic rendition of U2's "Desire." She hadn't needed to enchant them. It was two weeks before Christmas, and she was in a magnanimous mood and eager to complete her latest assignment, especially since it involved setting foot inside the most god-hospitable bar in the southwestern United States.

The Irish pub known as Glandomirum was superficially Irish. It was located a mere tankard's throw from the I-15, which stretched parallel with Las Vegas Boulevard where it meets Tropicana Avenue. In Glandomirum, the shabbier Celtic divinities hashed out their disagreements and blood-signed covenants. The bar served as neutral ground for a neutrality-challenged pantheon. But the bright charge of malted barley tended to heal all rifts—including the persistent wounds of rape and murder—and no one brewed tastier, more tranquilizing beer than Goibhniu. Maybe it was because he laced his product with hensbane. Maybe it was the heated metamorphic rocks—chipped from the Callanish stone circle in Scotland—that he plopped into a ditch of liquefied malt during the brewing process. Maybe it was nostalgia for the Iron Age.

Whatever the reason, Airmid swore that a goblet of Goibhniu-crafted ale could sweeten even the sour heart of the war god Neit. The only flaw she and everyone else noticed was that the beer reeked of billy goat's bum. Still, they happily guzzled.

Goibhniu was wiping down the bar when Airmid sat down on a stool. He didn't need to look up to know there was an ancient deity in his establishment. The place was unusually slow because of the rain. A pool table surrounded by college kids in UNLV shirts while watching a basketball game on the TV screens was the only action.

She remained silent, patiently waiting for Goibhniu to finish. He never charged his fellow gods, but he didn't rush to serve non-payers.

Finally, he poured two glasses of his signature malt from a stand-alone tap situated far away from the putrid commercial dregs he served to tourists.

"Lovely Airmid," he said, placing a chalice in front of her. "It's been too long. How's business?"

"Thank you, kind sir. Business is slow when everyone behaves. I have less to do, but I can't resent a lasting peace."

"Well," he replied, "as my customers say this time of year: Peace on earth." He toasted her.

They sipped, Airmid savoring the mugwort, carrot seeds, and nightshade. Together they provided a dark, smoky color and taste.

"Your beer gets better over the centuries," she said.

He ignored her praise. "You suggest everyone is behaving. Can't be true if you're here."

She licked foam from her lip. "I'm here because of Fintan."

Goibhniu stiffened his back and folded his arms. "He was here yesterday, of course. But I'm not hiding him."

"Never crossed my mind."

There was a lengthy silence. Airmid knew she wasn't at all intimidating. She had the soft, feathery physique of a postwar North American torch singer. Which is why she sang five nights a week in Las Vegas. But her ability to heal the deepest wounds—including those induced by Balor's incinerating cranium rays—gave her status.

Eventually, Goibhniu leaned forward to take a swig and said, with empathy in his ragged blacksmith voice: "You know, maybe it wasn't a good idea, putting Fintan in a cave with fifty women. It made him feel a little… how can I put this?"

"Henpecked?" she said.

Goibhniu nodded.

Airmid shrugged. "Old news. Besides, how else was Ireland supposed to repopulate after the flood?"

"Have *you* ever tried it? Impregnating an entire platoon of ovulating banshees?"

She sighed, the beer so delicious it kept her from rolling her eyes. "*That* I have not. So where is he, then?"

"Says he's staying at the Golden Nugget. He thinks he's a salmon again."

"I went there before my gig. He checked out last night."

"He likes the pool. It has a giant shark aquarium in the middle of it. It's really the best place for swimming in this town. We have an aquarium over there, but it's freshwater. But maybe it's enough for Fintan." Goibhniu indicated a hefty thirty-gallon tank near the cigarette machine that contained a few blue-backed, silver bass—a sport fish found in estuarine backwaters from Galway to Dublin. They looked bored.

"Swimming," she repeated. "Salmon."

"Yes. He came in here with that expression on his face he had back when—well, back when the Jewish god turned on the faucet and forgot to shut it off."

"In the desert."

"What?"

"Salmon in the desert."

"Airmid, your tolerance is shot. You should drink here more often, not just—"

She snapped her fingers suddenly, which caused Goibhniu to turn around and head back to his special beer tap.

"No!" she insisted. "Hoover Dam."

"We don't carry that."

She waved away his confusion. "The dam is where he's going, if he's not there already."

Goibhniu rubbed his long, grey-streaked beard. "Huh. That's good. I see now why they pay you for this." He meant the informal association of the Celtic immortals, who routinely hired Airmid as a fixer to remedy their day-to-day—or century-to-century—woes. She was a slender enchantress, an unassuming medic, and, when things got hairy, a cunning resurrector of the dead.

But not of her deceased sibling Miach.

"I don't get paid," she corrected. "They let me sit at the grave of my brother, and we get to talk for a few days before he turns to rot again."

There was another prolonged silence, until finally the billiard balls cracked and there was unrelated laughter, a joke shared among university chums. Goibhniu chose that moment to clear his throat and asked Airmid to please join him in toasting the memory of Miach, her brother, slain by their hideous and evil father.

She drained her glass. Teary, she thanked Goibhniu and left Glandomirum to hop into her Nissan Altima and sleep before driving to the waters of Hoover Dam.

Before that, though, she needed to stop at PetSmart to pick up a glass fishbowl.

♣

The rain was coming down in sheets, and the traffic was terrifying. It had been a few years since Airmid had visited the dam. But once she pulled in to the visitor's center from the Nevada side, she recalled her delight in the spectacle of the penstock towers, the sprawling spillway entrance, and the Mike O'Callaghan-Pat Tillman Memorial Bridge. She always enjoyed pagan displays of masculine strength and self-sacrifice, and this was among the best that mortals had ever constructed. She especially relished the fact that more than 100 of them had given their lives to complete this monolithic, nature-reversing monstrosity nearly a century ago.

"Such dedication," she murmured aloud, parking the car and digging in her back seat for a Harrah's umbrella.

Airmid walked through the exhibit's gallery of Depression-era murals and maps and into the darkened auditorium. A documentary devoted to the Bureau of Reclamation and its taming of the rivers was playing to a small number of spectators, one of whom as Fintan. She quietly sat a few seats away from the delinquent, shape-shifting Gaelic god, listening to the authoritative man's voice drone on about how the federal government contributed to help settle the West and grow the food that fed a nation.

Movie over, the lights came up and the sparse audience exited. Airmid and Fintan sat alone in the theater, not sharing words. She noted how much Fintan resembled Mr. Clean, a brand name and mascot for a chemical company. She had used the stuff recently to mop the dog hair and spaghetti sauce from her condo floor.

Finally, Fintan said: "When the waters rushed over the land and the mortals all drowned, I would've done anything to make it stop. I would've given my life."

"It wasn't up to you," said Airmid. "You never had a choice."

"I could've used a dam like this one. To redirect the water."

"Redirect it where?"

"Down the throat of that obnoxious fisherman from Galilee. The fisher of men whose big, unhappy daddy flooded the world." He meant, of course, Jesus.

"You're misremembering. Dude hadn't been born at that point. He didn't appear until you had changed from a hawk into a man and fought at Magh Tuireadh."

Fintan leaned forward, elbows on his thighs, to rub his furrowed brow. "I was covered in blood the entire time. I didn't hear of Jesus until Pelayo stopped the Moors at Covadonga."

Airmid snickered. "I always liked those Visigoths. They were fussy as hell—until you really needed them. And then they'd kill everyone to help a friend."

"Speaking of friends," said Fintan. "They sent the only woman I can stomach at this point to bring me back. But I'm still not going."

"You *have* to. You can't be a salmon. Such a waste to end up as bear food!"

"I'm not food," he said, and as his form began to expand and hair sprouted from his bald head and fangs appeared in his mouth. "I *am* the bear."

Airmid stumbled out of her seat and struggled to get clear of his massive claw, which came swinging at her like a battle axe. He'd nearly lopped her face clean off.

Seven feet in height now, his bulk expanded so quickly that the plastic seats around him splinter-cracked into flying pieces. He roared deafeningly, close enough that his gross grizzly spittle splattered her jeans.

She popped open her umbrella. "*Gaoithe*," she said. Nylon canopy inverted, the metal ribs began spinning rapidly, causing a wind-tunnel effect that caught Fintan off guard, the skin of his snout distorted by the force of compressed air.

He uttered a bear-like grunt of surprise, took a step backward, and fell over a piece of broken furniture with a bone-crunching thud that made Airmid wince.

Because she wasn't sure of the extent of his anger, she quickly closed the distance between them and ripped the fabric from the umbrella so she could wield the sharpened ferrule like a dagger and bring him to heel with a few non-fatal stabs. But he had already reverted to humanoid form, curled in the fetal position, clothes shredded and mostly useless from his sudden transformation. He wept.

"Fintan," she said. "Stop crying."

The auditorium was empty save the two of them, and the lights dimmed. The docu-film began playing again, opening with black-and-white newsreel footage of the series of dynamite explosions that eventually pushed the Colorado River's flow around the dam construction site and through the walls of Black Canyon. The theater's sound system was top-notch, the enhanced detonations rattling Airmid's teeth in her skull.

"I don't want to go back," blubbered Fintan, after the detonation sequence subsided.

"You're not going far. And it won't be long."

"The water. There's just too much water."

"*Ah-bur areesh aye.*"

"So— so why do we have to drown?"

"The world is parched, dry as a shite in the desert. Every now and again you have to add dilutables or else it all gets stuck, see?"

"No, I *don't* see. Help me, Airmid. Please don't let them— "

Suddenly Fintan was spotlit; he cringed like a vampire in the sun.

"What the hell happened in here?" A private-security guard hired by the dam had lit them up with his flashlight. "Did you cause this damage, ma'am?"

"*Aisling*," she said, and the guard stood stock-still and silent. His beam remained frozen on her, so she raised her arm to shield herself from the glare.

She turned to command Fintan to follow her outside, but he was gone.

She ran furiously, catching sight of him in the parking lot. He was sprinting for his car, and *damn* he was fast, faster than a *mac tíre* dancing across greased coals.

"*Cuir ar foluain*," she said, and her mutilated umbrella sprung to life, helicopter-launching her above the rows of vehicles like some improper Mary Poppins.

She landed a few yards in front of him, and he skidded, planting his feet to switch direction. But she guessed his move and roundhouse-kicked him, the heel of her purple-glittered APL TechLoom Pro Sneakers crushing his jaw.

Flat on his back on the asphalt, he groan-gasped in pain. "Where'd you learn how to kick like that, Airmid?"

"Las Vegas," she said, a little out of breath, "is a big MMA town."

When Airmid walked into Glandomirum for the second time in twenty-four hours, she carried a fishbowl with a single fish inside it. Goibhniu was soaking the bar gun in a pitcher of club soda while biting into a corned-beef sandwich, pieces of shredded cabbage falling off. The Proclaimers' "500 Miles" was pumping through the speakers, a song that normally filled her with dread, but it sounded great at the moment, having secured her quarry. Soon—probably tomorrow—she'd be chatting with her dead brother.

"That Fintan?" said Goibhniu through a mouthful of meat and bread.

"In the scaly flesh," said Airmid, plopping the bowl on the mahogany bar top.

"Was he agitated?"

"A little. He turned into a bear and nearly decapitated me."

Goibhniu guffawed. "He's all bark. A little dog can startle a hare, but it takes a big one to catch it."

"Wait," said Airmid. "Are you calling me a dog or a bunny?"

He laughed again. Then he thought about it a moment, and shrugged. "What's your next step?"

"We'll keep him in your aquarium, I think. Until we can be sure this isn't a broken agreement." She indicated the growing storm outside. The traffic lights were all blinking red from Boulder City to Las Vegas, and the Strip was down to one lane from the flooding. The casino signage lost its glow in the inclement gloam.

Goibhniu squinted, trying to make out the chaos through the windows of his bar. "Think it's the big one?"

Airmid shrugged. "Not sure. I mean, there's global warming, melting icebergs and such. But maybe it's just plain-ol' Old Testament rain."

He gestured toward the fish in the bowl. "Hope he's up for it."

"Ha! He did a fine job last time," she said. "The Irish and Scots are great fighters."

"Great artists, too," Goibhniu added, raising an eyebrow.

"Lovers."

"And legendary drinkers!"

"I'll drink to *that*," said Airmid.

Goibhniu went to the tap and poured them each a glass of ancient Gaelic ale.

They sat across the bar from each other and pitied the poor soon-to-spawn fish and listened to rain blanketing the concrete-stricken desertscape. He dreamed of her pale, creamy thighs; she dreamed of her brother's cherry lips.

It came down for a very long time.

# SALTED EARTH

*Willow Croft*

This damp was the dampness of earth. Not the clean wet of the ocean. This was musty worm damp. The basement had been their headquarters for months, yet Michael still couldn't get used to the rank smell. He settled into his seat while the young ones flashed messages at each other through their phones. It annoyed him, but the cause needed as many fighters as it could get. And he was worried. Would they even want to return to traditional life after being exposed to this fast-paced, exciting world?

Sarah walked into the room, rolls of paper under her arm. The young ones put their phones away. A good sign, Michael thought.

"Stage Three." Sarah began unrolling the papers and taping them up on the stained wall. "The final stage. And the most difficult."

"More difficult than freeing animals from their enslavement in zoos and in people's homes?"

"Yes, child, I'm afraid so." Sarah smiled at a girl in the front row. "You will need to be braver than ever."

"They are calling us terrorists," a young man with spiky blue hair said. "They are saying that if they catch us, we will be executed."

Sarah met Michael's eyes over the heads of the team. Time for a pep talk, her look said.

"Team." Michael stood up and held out his hands. "It is they who are the terrorists. They who are the criminals. Please, remember why we are here. They have started this war. Waged war not only against each other, but against those without voices. Not only animals, but trees. Rivers. And the ocean, from which life came, and without which life cannot continue. To not carry this through means a worse betrayal than any of our enemies have committed. For we act in love; a divine love. Her love, her life that flows through all creation."

Michael nodded to Sarah as a quiet murmuring spread through the crowd. He sat down and reaffirmed his own vow.

He heard the slap of the pointer against the paper and opened his eyes.

"The BioCorridor." Sarah announced. "Its hub is based here in Glasgow. The perfect symbol of our enemy's audacity to act with the authority of the divine. To challenge the nature of creation itself. To not only act as creator but as divine destroyer as well. To hold the strings of fate in their feeble hands, and pass judgment on who lives or dies, under their guise of promoting medical advancement and innovation. This is our final target."

The girl in the front row raised her hand.

"Yes, Natalie?"

"But, if we target them, aren't we also taking on the authority of the divine?"

Sarah smiled. "How proud I am of your cleverness. You are right. Let me explain further." Sarah pointed to a photo on the wall. The structures in the photo glowed with greens and blues against the night sky. "Within these buildings are victims, sacrifices on the altar of our enemy's arrogance. Animals subjected to cruel tests. Torture. Abuse. Atrocities that you cannot even imagine." Sarah paused. "And this is why I have to ask you to be braver than ever. The things you will witness in these buildings are the stuff of nightmares. Of demons. There is nothing I can do to prepare you for what you will see. Only give you these." She pulled a blanket off of a box. In the box were weapons: rifles, handguns, knives. A collective gasp broke out among the crowd.

Michael added; the soft touch to Sarah's sternness, "Take solace, dear ones, in that real healing awaits these victims. Not the mock healing our enemy peddles in forms of poisonous pills and ineffectual treatments, but true healing. And she will be the one to exact the final retribution against our enemy, not us. These weapons that you see before you are for our protection, not to cause harm. Sarah tells me the complex we are entering is heavily secured, and you'll need to defend yourselves."

"Training begins tomorrow. After morning meal." Sarah added. "Meeting adjourned."

The team was quiet as they filed out of the basement and back to their rooms upstairs. Michael watched as Sarah sank into the closest chair.

"The team's one thing—what about you? Are you going to make it?" Michael put his hand on her shoulder.

"Like I told the team, we're almost through this." Sarah took his hand in hers and held it tight enough to make it tingle. "I can't hear her, lately. It's too noisy here. How can they stand it? All machines and bright lights and music and people yelling all the time. Sometimes I feel she's abandoned us, too."

"She hasn't."

"I wish I had your faith. I'm the warrior, you know, I follow orders. You're the believer, priest."

"I don't need to just believe this time. I know. I've seen it."

"Seen what?"

"The river is rising. She's out there, and, it seems, her plaid is dirtier than usual."

Sarah shivered. "And, with that, I need a drink. And not one of those syrupy coffee things the young ones like."

"Certainly, boss," Michael said, pulling her up and giving her a kiss before they headed out into the loud, bright night.

♣

A week later, and their special ops team was ready.

"Well, if by ready, they can at least hold onto their weapons without dropping them," Sarah whispered into Michael's ear.

*Ready or not, at least it's the last time I have to smell this basement*, Michael thought. But Sarah was nervous enough, so he didn't whisper his thoughts back.

"Natalie, you take the lead. Alan, rear flank. Keep weapons under wraps until we gain access to the buildings. As far as anyone knows, we're just a pub crawl. Or so the signs on the vans say. Act like drunk tourists."

Michael waited until the boy with the spiky blue hair took his position. He blessed each team member in turn, calling them by their real names when invoking the protection of the *Cailleach Bhéara.*

"Let's load up," Sarah told her team, sounding impatient. She hung back, packing up her own bag with her ammunition.

Michael saw her hands tremble slightly. He held them until they stopped, then said a blessing for her, too.

Sarah handed him a handgun. "Just in case," she said. "Now move it."

The air inside the van was already filling up with the smell of salt as Michael climbed into the driver's seat. *Sweat*, Michael realized. They were all nervous. The smell was comforting, though, like the ocean was all around him.

He followed the other two vans, and they were at the complex before he knew it. Michael opened the door, and scattered beer bottles around on the pavement, as a disguise. As planned the vans had parked front to back, providing a screen for loading the animals in the crates.

Sarah came up and tapped him on the shoulder. "Cameras are down. Follow me." Then she said in a slightly louder voice. "Remember, team, shoot to disarm only, if you can."

They moved through the shadows, avoiding the pools of light scattered throughout the parking lot. Two of the teams split off to the other buildings. Michael waited, holding his breath, while Sarah used the keycard on the door. It beeped green and Sarah pulled open the door.

"Take the rear, now," Sarah said, as she gestured for the team to take flanking positions.

Michael noticed a flickering light coming from the right. Sarah held up her hand and her team froze. She edged up to the source of the light and looked around the corner. She crouched down and crawled along the floor. Her team followed her action. Michael could hear the sound of a television coming from the room they were crawling past. Someone was yelling at the television. Michael kept crawling. His foot thumped against the wall. The yelling stopped. Ahead of him, he saw Sarah stand up and lift her weapon.

"No, no, no," he heard two voices yell, in unison. Sarah motioned for him to start crawling, and, by the looks of it, she wanted him to do it fast.

It still seemed to take him forever, and every squeak his shoes made against the floor shot fear into his chest.

Sarah used her keycard on another door. This one slid open with a hiss. "You're up, priest." She shoved him into the room. Dogs started barking and he could hear, further down the row, the sound of monkeys screaming and banging on bars.

"Hurry," she said.

Michael quickly chanted a quieting spell. Almost instantly, the animals ceased talking.

"Well, at least you're good for something. If that gentling spell works, I'll forgive you for nearly alerting the guards, earlier." Sarah ordered her team to start removing the animals from the cages.

"Where's the rest of the guards? You said this place was supposed to be heavily guarded."

Sarah shoved a couple of half-shaved rabbits into his arms. "Local football game."

"I don't understand…"

"I'll explain later."

Michael helped their team carry animals back to the van. The ones in quarantine were the worst looking. His eyes burned, and he tried to blink away the tears. His weren't the only red eyes on the team. And the boy with the spiky blue hair threw up while carrying a cat with wires coming out of its head.

"It's okay," Sarah said. Michael had never heard her speak so gently. "I'll take her; she's the last one. Go to the van and get cleaned up."

"It's over," Michael said. "We did it."

"Not yet," Sarah said, putting the cat into a crate. It let out a soft meow. "Out of Glasgow and to Fintry."

"Where we await the Cailleach." The ground rumbled beneath Michael's feet.

"Speaking of…" Sarah slammed the door. "Hurry," she yelled to the other two teams. "Get the last of the animals. We leave now."

A few young ones came running up, handfuls of mice in their hands and more trying to squirm their way out of their pockets.

Michael would have laughed except a siren started blaring. Red lights flashed all around them.

"I'm driving." Sarah grabbed the keys from him. "You start praying."

And Michael did just that. Prayed as police cars flew past them. Prayed as they wound around Glasgow's streets until they got on the main motorway out of Glasgow. Prayed as they got on the winding road to Fintry.

"Okay, you can stop praying now. We're safe. We did it."

Michael opened his mouth to answer her only to discover that he was too tired to speak. *This must be what being human feels like.* He wished he had one of those coffee drinks. His head filled with a strange buzzing noise and then everything went soft and black.

"Home." A faraway voice said.

"Home," Michael said, smiling. He rolled over and felt the seatbelt pushing against his cheek. He sat up. "We're not home."

Sarah tugged him from the passenger seat.

"The animals. How are they?"

"Healed. And blessed."

"Glasgow?"

"Underwater. Currently being cleansed by the River Clyde."

"We did it."

"Well…"

Michael sighed.

"Where next?"

"Dublin. But first…"

And then Michael smelled it. The faintest hint of salt. He was imagining it, he knew. But then he heard it. And that wasn't his imagination.

Horses. Horses splashing in the water. And singing to the faraway ocean.

"...it's time to go home," Sarah finished.

# LADY OF THE CROWS

*Laila Amado*

I am Jane Doe. In all probability, I had a different name before the accident, but this memory was taken from me, along with all the others. Hell, I don't even remember the accident. No idea why the doctor insists on seeing me every six months. If I were to recover even one measly scrape of memory, I'd come running to see him myself. As it is, I travel by subway across town to get my pulse taken by a pudgy old nurse and go back to the halfway house in a crammed rush hour train.

The train rocks and sways. Bodies press against each other. In a crowded tunnel a couple of soldiers elbow their way through the throng, pushing me into the path of an old beggar woman. Where are they off to in such a hurry?

I press a coin into the crone's palm and flinch when she grabs my wrist. Her voice comes in a rustle of dry leaves, "I take no charity - only fair exchange." A black feather lands in my hand and she is gone, obscured by the crowd.

I marvel at the feather, its silhouette a perfect dark blade, as the crowd carries me up the stairs, pushes through the gate, and spits me out into the labyrinth of red brick and concrete.

I dive into the empty back alley leading to the halfway house, but only manage a few steps when a sudden noise makes me flinch - up on the fire escape a giant crow is beating its wings. It cocks its head, one intelligent beady eye staring at me, and I can swear I can hear it say, "You have something that belongs to me."

The old beggar's words sound in my ears and, tightening my grip on the feather, I say, "No charity. Only fair exchange. What would you give for it?"

The bird edges closer. "What would you like to have?"

"My memory back."

The crow squints at me. "Are you sure? You so wanted it gone."

"I want it back!"

The black bird cackles. In my memory there is a murder of crows, there are houses burning and fields on fire, there are screams and bleeding flesh. Pain drives me to my knees and the bird says, "Welcome back, Morrigan. You are right on time. Looks like someone has just started a war."

In the distance a siren wails. One, then another.

# DRUIDS OF MONTREAL

*I. E. Kneverday*

## Part I: A Clairvoyant Woman Walks into an Irish Pub

A clairvoyant woman walks into an Irish pub and before you even ask, no, this isn't the beginning of some joke or drunken tale told by an idiot—this is precisely what happens. She walks into an Irish pub, my pub, sits down on the barstool right next to mine, orders a vodka soda with lime from Rory, and proceeds to tell me that my "colors" are bleak.

"Thank you?" I say, unsure if this is the proper etiquette for acknowledging such a compliment, or insinuation, or whatever it is I'm dealing with here.

It's at this point I notice that her hair is impeccably dark and meticulously coiffed. Streamlined. Not a single coil of fuzz extending from its flawless sheen.

"You must think I'm crazy," she says next, presumably reading my thoughts. "But the truth is I don't tell many people about my gift. It's just that, tonight… well, you know."

At that, she gives a ceremonial nod toward her vodka soda with lime. Picks it up. Takes a sip.

"Oh, *I* know," I say, stupidly, before taking a nervous gulp from my pint of stout.

I try to lock eyes with Rory, who's at the far end of the bar. I'm desperate for a conversational lifeline. But it's Hockey Night in Canada and the Ontario-born barkeep is watching his Leafs take a thumping on the ancient TV that's chained up in the corner.

"What's your name?" the woman asks, recapturing my gaze.

"Finn," I say, suppressing the urge to make her guess. "What's yours?"

"Finn," she echoes, ignoring the second half of my response. "And what are you doing here, Finn?"

"Believe it or not, I'm the weekend busboy," I say, tapping the bottom of my glass on the bar. "Slow night."

"I meant in Montreal."

"Oh, uh, I'm a student."

"A student of what?"

"Well, uh, I'm undecided at the moment."

"Of course you are," she says, not in a venomous way, but certainly not in a nice way either.

I take another nervous gulp from my pint of stout.

♣

Five minutes later, the clairvoyant woman is walking out of the pub, her high heels clacking like raptor talons on the tiled floor of the front hallway. I carry her empty glass behind the bar, squeeze some pink dish soap out of a repurposed yellow mustard bottle, turn on the hot water, then run my thumb and forefinger ever-so-gently around the edge of the glass to clean off the lipstick stains she's left behind.

"It's about time you got back to work," Rory barks, still facing the TV.

"Yeah yeah yeah," I play along. "I've really let the place go to hell."

Apart from Rory and I, there are now only three other people in the pub: Shane, our resident musician (who's yet to play a set), and a pair of regulars.

The TV flashes and an angry man in a floral-pattern suit appears on the screen. Hockey Night in Canada will return after these messages, he promises, before yielding the airwaves to an advertisement for farm-raised Vancouver salmon. And just like that, Rory's trance is broken. He dances his way behind the bar, arms swinging in excitement—his Leafs are only down by a goal.

"So, what did she say to you?" he asks, slapping a friendly hand on my shoulder.

"You mean the crazy woman?"

Rory furrows his brow.

"You think she's… unwell in some way?"

"I mean, she said she could read my colors. And that they were 'bleak.'"

Rory scratches at the golden-orange bristles covering his chin.

"Funny. I remember her coming in here a couple years ago, before your time. And I'm pretty sure she said the same exact thing to me. And to Shane."—he looks around the pub—"Oh, and to Gabrielle and Marie-Jeanne."

"Wait, seriously?" I gasp, my ego flailing with the realization that the clairvoyant woman had once had the audacity to diagnose *other people* with this affliction of the aura, an infliction that I had at first thought, so naively, to be uncommon.

"I would never lie about such important matters," says Rory.

"So… she is crazy," I deduce, unintelligently.

"Or maybe everyone who drinks in this pub has a tortured soul," Rory says with a smile as he reaches for a pair of shot glasses.

♣

An hour and several shots of whiskey later, Rory and I are sitting in a booth competing in a no-limit Texas hold 'em tournament with Shane the musician (who still hasn't played a set) and the two regulars: Gabrielle, a waitress and cocaine enthusiast from the jazz club up the street, and Marie-Jeanne, an underwater welder who spends her days submerged in the frigid St. Lawrence making sure the city's bridges don't collapse and that the island of Montreal—and it *is* an island, something I didn't learn until moving here last year—remains connected to the rest of the world.

Without warning, Rory goes all-in, gets called, and is soon all-out, much to Shane's delight. But alas, much to Shane's chagrin, Rory pulls a fresh twenty from his wallet and promptly buys back in, pointing out, correctly, that a "no rebuy" rule had not been established prior to the start of tournament play.

The table decrees, after a 4-1 vote, that a "one rebuy" rule shall henceforth be in effect for the rest of the tournament. And really, this is a measure designed to protect Rory, not punish him.

Rory, whose pupils have grown a full centimeter wider since an hour ago.

Rory, whose body odor has grown exponentially stronger in that timeframe as well. That, of course, being one of Rory's many quirks. Having grown up in a steel town, he refuses to "defile" his body by applying aluminum-derived products to his armpits.

"Have I ever told you guys the knife story?" Rory is asking now while stacking his newly acquired chips into tiny, leaning towers.

"Yes, Rory, we've all heard the knife story," I imagine us replying in unison like some dysfunctional sitcom family. Meanwhile, in reality, some of us grunt, some of us nod, but otherwise, we ignore him, opting instead to focus on our cards.

Except for Marie-Jeanne, that is.

"Actually, Rory, now that you mention it, I don't think I've heard—"

"Let's go! Big blind, small blind, fuckers," Shane shouts, interrupting her. "You can't forget to put those in."

Gabrielle drops a pair of chips onto the table. The ceramic colliding with the wood produces a satisfying *clack*. "Hey, don't be such a fucker, fucker," she says to Shane.

Shane's cheeks are Santa-Claus red. Brown and grey strands of '70s-rock-star hair are plastered to his forehead, like seaweed strewn over a rock. He smiles. An unexpectedly cherubic smile. A smile that instantly makes him look years younger. Then he puts out his fist.

Gabrielle smiles back.

Pounds his fist with her own.

"So, I needed some new knives," Rory continues as if there had been no interruption. "Some good kitchen knives, you know? Because mine had become all rusty and I couldn't sharpen them for the life of me. So, one night, and I happened to be completely wasted that night—"

"Surprise, surprise," Marie-Jeanne chimes in.

"Yeah yeah yeah," says Rory. "So, anyway, I walk into this restaurant, that nice Italian place over on *Saint-Laurent*, you know the one? Caggiano's or Reggiano's or something like that. Hey, did you hear they can't call pasta 'pasta' on their menu anymore? They have to call it '*pâtes*' now because the OQLF came in and—"

"Rory," Shane snaps. "It's on you."

"Okay, okay. Jesus, I call. So, where was I? Right, so, I walk into this restaurant and I'm completely wasted and I see that there's no one in the kitchen, you know? There's no one back there. So I walk into the kitchen and there's this knife rack on the wall with all of these amazing knives. Butcher knives and chef knives and all sorts of knives. So I start sticking these knives down my pants. Or in my belt, you know? I start tucking them in there. And then I hear someone behind me yelling, 'Hey, turn around! What the hell are you doing?' And I say, 'Okay, I'm gonna turn around but I have to tell you that I took some of your knives and they're in my pants.' So I turn around and the guy sees that I have like a dozen knives, a baker's dozen, probably, sticking out of my belt and he just gives me an odd look and starts laughing and calls for the manager."

"Did you get arrested?" I ask.

"No no no. I put all the knives back and they let me go."

"Fucking idiot," Shane says, folding his hand.

♣

After more shots and pints and a cigarette in the alleyway, one foot in the door, keeping an eye on the table, another shot and another pint and lighting a second cigarette with the first and another pint and then… there are just two players left:

Rory and Shane.

Two celestial bodies that had been destined to collide from the start. Both bodies full of alcohol, but only one showing any sign of it.

Rory is swaying rhythmically back and forth as if his chair is mounted to the deck of an invisible ship. His eyes are as wide as I've ever seen them.

Shane goes all in.

Rory calls.

Rory wins.

The game is over.

Shane screams a string of obscenities, the closest he's come to singing all night, then quietly threatens murder while Rory smiles what can only be described as a goofy goddamn smile and stands up on wobbly legs to collect his winnings.

"Shots!" he declares proudly after stuffing six twenty-dollar bills, two of which had been his own, into his wallet. "Shotsforeveryone!"

Shane doesn't participate. Instead, he storms the pub's tiny corner stage, grabs his guitar by the neck, shoves it into his gig bag, and leaves.

Meanwhile, Gabrielle and Marie-Jeanne congregate at the end of the bar in anticipation of the aforementioned shots and begin commentating on the (arguably) surprising outcome of tonight's impromptu poker game.

"*Tabarnak! Je ne le crois pas.*"

"I can't believe it either!"

"*C'est incroyable.*"

"It's a goddamn miracle is what it is."

"Or just plain luck," I mutter, ever the sore loser.

We down our shots and I toss the glasses in the sink while Rory begins jabbing at the oversized plastic buttons of a desktop calculator. Jumbled ribbons of receipts litter the bartop around him.

If there's order in this chaos, it's well-disguised.

I'm worried Rory isn't going to be able to finish his cash. Worried that by the time we walk out of this place the sun will be shining and the day staff will be walking in. But just as I'm preemptively blaming Rory for this potential inconvenience, I see his golden-orange eyebrows shoot skyward.

"Finn," he calls. "Fiiinn!" Louder this time. "Ditchoo... Ditchoo lockthefrontdoor?"

"Shit."

Completely forgot.

I grab the key from behind the bar and sprint toward the front entryway. The worn-out soles of my shoes allow me to slide across the tiled floor like it's an iced-over pond.

Upon hearing the familiar *clink* of the lock, a wave of calm washes over me.

With the door locked, there's no longer a risk of late-night rabble-rousers or miscreants or other unsavory characters crossing that threshold and causing us trouble. And, more importantly, it means that Rory can now smoke inside.

♣

Blue tendrils escape from Rory's Number 7 and creep ceilingward as I wipe down tables that are already clean and hum songs that Shane never bothered to play tonight.

Gabrielle and Marie-Jeanne are presently polishing off their last-call pints and chattering aggressively (about what, I am unable to understand). I flash them a sheepish, don't-mind-me smile as I glide around the pub on tired legs, working through my end-of-night checklist.

Passing the stage, I see that the illuminated stained-glass sign hanging above it, the one that bears the pub's name, or at least, its English name, is still aglow. On numerous occasions, the *Office Québécois de la Langue Française* has threatened to remove it, along with all of the English-language posters and paraphernalia covering the pub's walls. But thus far, the OQLF's threats have remained empty. "It's amazing what a little old-fashioned palm-greasing can do," Rory had once offered by way of explanation.

I hop up onto the stage, pull the skinny, beaded chain, the kind you might find hanging from a basement light fixture, and "The Old Shamrock" fades out of existence.

Meanwhile, the employees of *Le Vieux Trèfle* need to keep burning that 4 a.m. oil.

Stepping off the stage, my foot kicks something, a plastic something, and sends it spinning. I bend down and pick up a small vodka bottle, empty, which must have fallen out of Shane's gig bag while he was packing up. I take the bottle out into the alleyway and shove it into the recycling bin, burying it deep below the surface.

♣

"HeyFinn. Fiiinn. Wannadoashot? Eh? Onemore? Beforewego?"

These are the sounds I awake to.

Eyes open, I unfold my arms, which had been crossed atop the bar, and as I do so, red crumbs begin flaking off my clammy flesh, falling like tiny dead leaves.

"Wannadoashot?" Rory asks again, his face beaming.

I flip open my cell phone and look at the time.

It's 5:07 a.m.

I search my memory. Replay locking up. Wiping down tables. Turning off the stained-glass stagelight. Taking out the trash and the recycling. Mopping the floors. Doubling up the kegs. Restocking the fridges. Saying "*bonne nuit*" to Gabrielle and Marie-Jeanne. Making a bad joke about it actually being morning. Promising Gabrielle that I'd make sure Rory didn't do anything stupid. Promising Marie-Jeanne that I'd make sure he got home safe. Watching the two of them stumble out, arm-and-arm, and being jealous that they were leaving. And that they were arm-and-arm. Then, slumping into a barstool. Chugging a glass of water. Devouring a bag of ketchup-flavored potato chips. Waiting. Waiting. Waiting.

"You finish doing your cash?" I ask.

I sound like a parent inquiring about the status of a child's homework. Only Rory is old enough to be *my* parent. And, technically, he's my boss. Both of these factors contribute to the awkwardness of the situation (at least in my mind).

"Yeahyeahyeah," Rory replies, oblivious to my inner turmoil. "Solet'sdoonemore, thenwego, yeah?

"No," I say, more loudly than I had expected to.

His smile turns to a sad-puppy frown.

"Justonemore. Beforewego," he whines, only he doesn't need to whine because he's already pouring the shots.

"Come on, man, it's late. I don't wanna do another shot."

"Yeahyeahyeah," he says, sliding the glass toward me.

"No no no," I reply. "I gotta get you home."

He raises an accusatory eyebrow. "Gottaget*me*home? Gottaget-*me*home? Whaddayou talkinabout?"

His agitation is palpable. I raise my glass.

"Let's just fuckin' do this."

And we cheers.

I bring the empty glasses to the sink. Turn on the tap. And, after making sure Rory isn't looking, spit whiskey down the drain.

We walk out of the pub.

♣

## Part II: "Needmoresmokes!"

"Needmoresmokes!" Rory repeats, more forcefully this time.

A trio of crows, which had been silently keeping their vigil atop a telephone wire, begin pumping their wings nervously, the *flap-flap-flap* of their feathers echoing off the asphalt.

"Yes, Rory, we're gonna stop so you can get smokes," I explain, again, before clarifying, "but *then* we're getting in a cab, remember?"

"Yeahyeahyeah."

We've been walking, or, in Rory's case, stumbling, for nearly five minutes, but have only succeeded just now in crossing the parking lot. Looking back over my shoulder, I can still see the pub, a green rectangle composed of smaller green rectangles, nestled among the steel and concrete monoliths that have come to dominate the city's skyline.

As we begin the slow trudge up the deceptively steep slope of *rue University*, it dawns on me that while my plan is to throw Rory in a cab (after he buys more smokes, of course), I don't actually know his address. While he's always the first person to show up at *your* apartment with a smile and a case of beer, Rory, unlike other members of the *Le Vieux Trèfle*'s staff, has never been one to host—not parties, not casual get-togethers, and not, heaven forbid, poker games. All I know is that he lives somewhere near campus, near the base of the city's namesake: *mont Royal.*

On any other night, or morning as it were, I'd eschew the cost of the cab and walk the mile back to my place in *Le Plateau*, leaving Rory to his own devices. But for some reason—maybe because I promised Gabrielle and Marie-Jeanne, or maybe because I'm worried about how I'd feel if something were to happen to him, *or* maybe because I'm genuinely concerned about his well-being, but probably because of some combination of all those things—I feel compelled to make sure Rory gets home.

Given the speed we're presently moving at, however, I can't be certain that I will ever actually succeed in that goal. And I can't help but think about how my charitable actions may end up disrupting the activities I had scheduled for later this morning—namely, going to Tam-Tams. Take one part drum circle, add equal parts arts & crafts fair and live-action role-playing tournament (during which adults and children alike dress in cardboard armor and attempt to de-limb each other with duct tape-covered foam weapons), and you'll have something approaching the free, open-air festival known as Tam-Tams, which takes place in *Parc du Mont-Royal* every Sunday. For a godless college student like myself, it's the closest thing I have to going to church, and thus far, my attendance record has been unblemished.

But will it remain that way?

"Needmoresmokes! Needmoresmokes!"

Rory's broken-record howling pulls me back to reality and I'm forced to reassess our present situation. Thankfully, we are now approaching the intersection of *rue University* and *rue Sainte-Catherine*, which means there will soon be plenty of 24-hour *dépanneurs* nearby where Rory can buy a pack of smokes.

From our new vantage point, I can see *mont Royal* looming ahead of us in the distance, a hulking mass of vegetation, dotted here and there with extravagant, castle-like stone structures. Of course, the most prominent feature of the mountain, some might say, is the glowing, one-hundred-foot-tall steel cross that punctuates its northeastern peak. Thanks to an advanced LED fiber-optic lighting system, which the cross dutifully bears upon its steel bones, city workers can change the cross's color—such as from white to purple, or purple to white, depending on what's happening with the Pope—with the push of a button.

At present, it's glowing green.

Really, the cross is the perfect symbol for this city, I think to myself. A little bit traditional, a little bit gaudy.

Paris meets Las Vegas.

I blink and see the naked body of a man suspended from this perfect symbol. Hair hanging down over his face. And what looks like a guitar slung over his shoulder.

I blink again and the cross is empty. Only the green LED lights remain, glowing like an "unoccupied" sign above an airplane bathroom.

"Did you just see that?" I gasp.

I turn to Rory, who is waiting to meet my gaze.

He smiles what can only be described as a goofy goddamn smile.

While Rory is inside the *dep* buying cigarettes, I'm waiting outside and quietly questioning my sanity, repeatedly daring myself to look at the cross to check if he's still there and repeatedly chickening out. I was always better at truth, anyway, I lie to myself.

I must be tired.

Over-tired is probably more accurate.

Heck, I fell asleep on the bar tonight. So, that settles it. That's what I'm going with. What I just experienced was your standard, run-of-the-mill, sleep-deprivation-induced hallucination of a pub musician being crucified.

Case closed.

Two minutes later, I hear raised voices coming from inside the *dep* and am about to go inside and investigate when Rory comes bumbling out, balancing five packs of cigarettes atop two open palms.

"Everything go alright in there?"

"Yeahyeahyeah."

I watch, admittedly with some degree of schadenfreude, as Rory struggles to stuff the cigarette packs into the front and back pockets of his pants.

"You stocking up or something?"

He ignores me.

There's a cab crawling down the street and I raise my hand to hail it, but Rory deftly sticks a cigarette between my fingers.

"Smokefirst, thenwego. Yeah?"

This hadn't been part of our original agreement, but it's something I should have anticipated. Not being in the mood to argue, and absolutely being in the mood for a smoke, I let the cab roll past.

We smoke in silence, standing on the sidewalk outside the *dep*, and all the while I'm wondering if the same, horrifying image that's flashing through my head is flashing through Rory's head as well. Just as I'm about to broach the subject, to ask him what he saw, to ask him what that goofy smile had been about, Rory speaks.

"I'mhungry. Youhungry?"

He gestures to the fast food joint across the street, its neon sign glowing yellow and red.

"Youwannagetsomething? Somethingtoeat?"

I flip open my phone.

It's 5:31 a.m.

My stomach rumbles.

♣

When it comes to reinvigorating the dulled senses of someone coming off a night shift, there's nothing quite like the caustic aroma of bleach and food-scented chemicals paired with the sterile, ocular onslaught provided by fluorescent lighting.

Rory and I are waiting in line, squinting up at the menu. It's busier than I had expected, although a lot of the people seated in the booths are catatonic, making the place feel eerily quiet, the soundscape consisting primarily of ragged breathing and sizzling oil.

"Ah fuckme," Rory howls, adding a new track to the mix.

Heads turn.

I look down to see that Rory has turned his pants pockets inside out. Cigarette packs and twenty-dollar bills litter the floor.

As I crouch down to help him scoop everything up, I contemplate the moral ramifications of taking a twenty for my troubles. A delivery fee, if you will, for getting him home safe (which, admittedly, I haven't done yet) and for covering the cost of a cab (which, admittedly, I haven't gotten for us yet). But my conscience forces me to abandon this disgusting idea, despite the fact, that, one of those twenties *had* been mine and had only come into Rory's possession by mere chance (or, at least, that's what I tell myself).

I begrudgingly hand everything back over to Rory.

"Adozencheesebugers," he declares upon reaching the front of the line, clumps of twenties in his hand. "Nonono, abaker'sdozen," he clarifies.

The woman behind the counter sticks to the script.

"Could you repeat that please, sir?"

"Isaid, Iwantabaker'sdozen. Ofcheeseburgers. *Douzainedeboungalers des* cheeseburgers."

This is the first time I've ever witnessed someone order a baker's dozen cheeseburgers. Or a baker's dozen anything, for that matter.

Oh, the pitfalls of drunken excess, I pontificate, assuming that at least half of those burgers will end up in the trash, uneaten, all because of some ridiculous impulse that had manifested in Rory's whiskey-logged brain.

My face is burning with embarrassment as I step forward to place my order. I consider pretending that I'm not with him, that he's just some random guy I bumped into when I got in line and that I just happened to be nice enough to help him pick up the money he had dropped (without stealing any of it, I might add).

Then, I remember we've both come directly from working at the pub, which means we're still in our matching uniforms: Black shoes. Black socks. Black slacks. Black t-shirts. We look like a couple of stagehands, I realize, before ordering a single cheeseburger and a side of fries and taking my place next to Rory, who's standing to the side of the counter.

No, not standing.

Dancing.

He's rocking back and forth, his hips swaying to the rhythm of some nonexistent song, or a song playing only in his mind. He's still dancing when he retrieves a paper bag containing a baker's dozen cheeseburgers from the cashier, grumbling a "*merci beaucoup*" as he does so. The bag looks over-stuffed, as if it is about to burst at the seams, and is nearly transparent on account of the grease.

♣

The plan had been to get in a cab.

The plan had been to go home.

Put as succinctly as possible, the plan had been to get in a cab and go home.

But then came the smokes. And the food. And, now, Rory refusing to get in a cab until we have eaten some of that food and have had a few more of those smokes.

So, here we are. Walking out the side entrance of the fast food joint. Turning down a side street. Searching for a place where we can eat and smoke and not get in a cab.

"Iknowagoodspot," Rory assures me.

But I don't feel assured. And I especially don't feel assured upon discovering that his "goodspot" is actually the Christ Church Cathedral.

The cathedral, which I must have walked by hundreds of times without ever really paying attention to before, is a fearsome-looking, gargoyle-infested remnant of the Gothic Revival movement. And, like *La Croix du mont Royal*, it's one of the city's most iconic religious structures.

"Hey, Rory," I finally work up the nerve to say as we step off the sidewalk and onto a well-trodden path. "I don't think we're supposed to be here."

Rory waves a hand.

"Meandyou, wecanbehere. It'sokay."

He scampers on ahead, his grease-saturated paper bag swinging back and forth by his side as he leads us past the cathedral's main entrance and around to a side courtyard. Along the way, we encounter piles of trash, murders of feasting crows, and the occasional human body rolled up in a sleeping bag. Amongst my other concerns, I'm concerned that there is not nearly enough distance between these three categories of things.

Ahead of us looms a stone archway, which mimics the ornate architecture of the cathedral's façade, complete with symmetrically arranged gargoyles, one on each side of its opening, and a stone cross topping its crown, centered above the keystone.

Standing at the threshold, I can see only darkness on the other side.

Well, darkness and branches.

## Part III: There Is Only One Tree in the Churchyard

There is only one tree in the courtyard, I realize now, standing on the other side of the archway, but it's the biggest tree I've ever seen.

Not the tallest, mind you, but the most expansive, the most sprawling, with dozens if not hundreds of horizontal limbs, thick as my torso, some thicker, crisscrossing the space beneath its opaque canopy, dividing the churchyard into chambers of various shapes and sizes.

In the beginning, all of these chambers are bathed in darkness.

Then, I see a flicker.

"There he is," Rory says, pointing. "Come on, I've got to introduce you to someone."

There's something about what Rory has just said that gnaws at me, but I can't quite put my finger on it. Then, as we're scrambling toward the light, crouching under some tree limbs and climbing over others, it hits me:

Rory has just spoken in complete, coherent sentences.

When I try to bring this peculiar fact to Rory's attention, however, a slew of garbled sounds spill from my mouth.

"Rooo... Rooo? Waaa? Ahhh?"

"Oh, right. *That,*" he says flatly. "You really shouldn't have spit out that last shot I gave you."

"Waaa-yooo… waaa-yoo-dooo?"

He waves a dismissive hand.

"Don't worry about it. I'm gonna have you all fixed up in no time."

The light that had once been flickering faintly in the distance soon reveals itself to be a bonfire, around which are seated about a dozen people.

I smell them before I can see them in any detail. The stench of sweat and soiled clothes. Of ancient fabrics crusty with biology. I want to turn around. I *am* turning around when Rory grabs me by the shoulder.

"What's up with you?"

I point to my nose.

"Nooo-gooo."

By way of reply, Rory smirks, inhales vigorously, his nostrils flaring with the effort, and then emits a deep, satisfied-sounding sigh, as if he'd just been huffing a hydrangea.

"Just wait," he says with a wink.

I wait, fuming in silence, listening to the murmurings of the men and women seated around the bonfire grow louder as we trudge ever forward. Beyond French and English, I can detect traces of German, Spanish, Italian, and what I think is Mandarin flowing from their mouths and out into the dank morning air. There's something undeniably soothing about their voices, about the way the different languages meld together, forming intricate chords and patterns—chords and patterns that Rory promptly smashes with his voice.

"Ogma, you old bastard!"

The multilingual murmurings come to a sudden halt.

A few unnerving seconds of silence pass by. Then…

"Rory, my boy!" a voice roars in response. "Is that you?"

"The one and only."

As we reach the edge of the bonfire, I see a bald, bone-thin man with ebony skin perched on a tree branch, just out of reach of the flames. The man's face is tattooed—a long strand of dark ink curving around his forehead, punctuated by a series of shorter, intersecting dashes. From this distance, it resembles a crown of barbed wire. Or thorns.

"And what have you brought for us this time, my good lad?" Ogma is asking now.

Rory casts a suspicious eye in my direction before hoisting his paper bag full of cheeseburgers aloft.

"Cheeseburgers," he proclaims. "Cheeseburgers for all."

The men and women sitting around the fire cheer and holler with gratitude as Rory begins handing out greasy, lukewarm balls of waxpaper-wrapped cheeseburgers. When the paper bag is empty, Rory reaches into his bulging pants pockets and pulls out the cigarette packs he'd bought earlier, rips them all open, and starts divvying up the cigarettes into little bundles.

"Here," he says to me. "Help me hand these out, will ya?"

I stare at him for a second, dumbfounded, then get to the task at hand, keeping my nose scrunched as I make my way around the circle.

"Who's your friend?" Ogma finally bothers to ask.

"Oh, right. That's Finn," Rory replies. "The weekend busboy. The one I was telling you about. From Boston."

"American?" Ogma snarls, before addressing me directly for the first time:

"*Parlez-vous français?*"

"Ehhh… Ehhh..." I mumble while rotating my hand, the universal sign for "a little bit." This, as it turns out, is exactly how I would have responded to the question were I still capable of speaking.

"Mmhmm. And what have *you* brought for us, Finn *l'Américain*?"

I take the single cheeseburger and single order of fries out of my bag and feel my face reddening.

If Rory had told me ahead of time that we were going to feed the homeless tonight I would've bought more food, I think to myself, trying to rationalize away the shame.

It doesn't work.

Ogma, a fresh coat of disgust now covering his face, looks to Rory.

"Is he supposed to be here?" he asks.

Rory hesitates.

"Yeah. I mean, I guess so. I mean, that's what Morrigan said."

"Morrigan?" Ogma moans. "That old crone?"

"Careful, Ogma, you're not getting any younger yourself, you know"

"Ah, but then what about you, Rory? You're no spring chicken either…"

As the two continue bickering, an idea coalesces in my brain.

I put my French fries together in little bundles, just like Rory had done with his cigarettes, then start walking around the bonfire and handing them out. When my French fry container is empty, the bickering stops.

"Get my friend a drink," Rory says to Ogma.

Both men are smiling what can only be described as goofy goddamn smiles.

♣

I look into the plastic cup and don't like what I see.

When Ogma had ladled it out of the metal pot, he had said it was a specialty mead of his own brewing. "Nectar of the gods," he had called it.

It's certainly an unfiltered mead, I consider, eyeing the yeast particles and rotten, hexagonal chunks of honeycomb floating listlessly about. Organic flotsam in a golden-brown sea.

I try to politely decline this generous offer with words but to no avail. Even uttering the most rudimentary of sounds now proves impossible. So, I put up a hand in protest. Shake my head. Make every physical gesture I can think of that signifies "no."

But Ogma is persistent.

"Drink," he says. "Drink of my mead, and you will know why they call me Ogma of the Honeyed Mouth. Drink of my mead, and you will know why they call me Ogma of the Sunny Countenance. Drink of my mead, and you will not only bear witness to the light shining through the cracks but shatter those partitions that keep our two worlds separate. Drink of my mead..."

While Ogma continues his recitations, Rory leans over and whispers in my ear.

"Just drink it," he says. "Trust me. It's good."

And I do trust him.

And it is good.

In fact, it's so good that after taking my first, teensy-weensy, just-in-case-it-might-be-poison sip, I tilt my cup back and begin gorging myself.

"There's a good lad," I just barely hear Ogma say over the sound of the sweet liquid surging down my gullet.

The flavor is so bright, so pure, so radiant. Like distilled sunlight. Or lava that has cooled but somehow been kept liquid—the energy of the Earth's core trapped in every sip.

"Hey," I say, wiping my mouth, "This is actually pretty good," only realizing several seconds later, after draining the rest of the cup's contents, that I've regained the power of speech.

But that's not all that's changed.

For starters, the odor that had been assaulting my nose and putting tears in my eyes? Gone. Replaced by the scent of apples and marigolds and crunchy autumn leaves. And as I lower the plastic cup from my lips and scan my surroundings, I see that there is no longer a single bonfire burning in the courtyard, but hundreds if not thousands of them, scattered beneath the branches of the biggest tree I've ever seen, illuminating entire populations of once-hidden people.

"Care for a refill?" Ogma asks.

Even while feeling the most confused I've ever felt in my entire life, even while hypothesizing that the stuff I just drank was laced with acid, or that I'm currently suffering from some kind of mental break, or, worst-case scenario, that I'm dead, I can't find it within myself to refuse Ogma's offer.

"Yes," I say, "I'd love a refill. But first, I have a question."

Ogma and Rory raise their eyebrows right on cue.

"Who's Morrigan?" I ask them.

After several more cups of mead and a cigarette from Rory and a cheeseburger and then another cup of mead and another cigarette from Rory, I'm nowhere closer to knowing who this Morrigan character is *but* I am definitely closer to feeling the happiest I've ever felt in my entire goddamned life so that's gotta count for something.

Then… I hear those words.

The words you never want to hear when you're feeling this Earth-shatteringly good:

"Alright, it's time to go."

"Go?" I reply. "But we just got here."

"Just got here?" Rory retorts. "Do you have any idea what time it is?"

I fish around in my pocket for my phone.

Flip it open.

Dead.

"We still have time for one more," I say, feigning confidence, and feigning it poorly.

"Finn." Rory pauses. Looks at me with an expression I've never seen on his face before—an expression of grave seriousness. "We have to go," he continues. "We've got people waiting for us."

"More people?"

"Yeah."

"At another bonfire?"

"Something like that."

"Do they have mead?"

Rory smiles.

"No. But they've got something better."

♣

A song is playing in 6/8 time.

An Irish song.

One of the old ones.

Its melody ripe with trills.

Its lyrics ripe with tales.

Of murder.

Of invading forces.

Of an island under siege.

Of a culture under threat of obliteration.

The song echoes throughout the cathedral-sized chamber I now find myself standing in, the vaulted ceiling of which is being supported by a massive, wooden spine. With my eyes, I follow the curve of the spine all the way down to its gnarled, bulging base, which is growing from the center of the chamber.

"Welcome," says Rory, "to the trunk."

The impossible trunk of the impossible oak is so wide that even after walking for several minutes in its direction, it appears no larger on the horizon.

The music, meanwhile, has been getting louder.

After another five minutes of walking, I discover its source:

Shane.

There he is, banging away on his old guitar, blood dripping from his hands.

He's sitting at the edge of a circular pool of water, which is about the size of your typical above-ground swimming pool, but unlike your typical above-ground swimming pool, there's a suspension bridge—

albeit a small one—stretching across it. There's also what looks like an aluminum rowboat resting on the pool's banks.

As Rory and I walk closer, I see Marie-Jeanne, in full scuba gear, swimming near the pool's surface, circling the bridge's foundations. The tip of a spear is poking up out of the water next to her.

Gabrielle is there, too. Sitting on the bridge's railing. Watching and giving direction to Marie-Jeanne from on high. Legs dangling.

Both of them are so absorbed in whatever it is they're doing that they don't see Rory and I approach.

"Hey, fuckers," Shane calls out, his song having reached its somber conclusion. "What are you doing here?"

"Same thing you're doing," Rory replies.

"Would one of you mind telling me what the hell is going on?" I interject, recognizing immediately upon doing so that the mood-elevating effects of Ogma's mead have all but dissipated. "Where the fuck are we? What is all this?"

I wave my hands wildly at the pool of water, at the bridge, at the rowboat, at the gargantuan, tapering tree trunk that is simultaneously right above us and miles away from us, even though I know that's not possible. Even though I know none of this is possible.

"You haven't told him yet?" Shane says to Rory.

"You have seniority," Rory replies. "I figured you'd want to do it. Now, if you'll excuse me, I have some business to attend to."

And with that, Rory walks over to the rowboat, drags it into the water, and hops aboard. Only now do I realize that the rowboat, of course, is made of steel, not aluminum.

"I'll see you later, Finn," Rory says, picking up a fishing rod that had been lying on the bottom boards. "We had a fun night, yeah?"

Then Rory's back is to me. And his fishing line is in the water.

I turn to Shane, who's been waiting to meet my gaze.

"What the fuck is happening?" I ask him. "Am I dreaming? Am I hallucinating? Am I… dead?"

"Chill out, you're not dead."

"Chill out? *Chill out?* Have you looked around you, Shane? This isn't normal. I mean, look at them. Look at *them*, right now. What the hell are they doing?"

"Fishing."

"Fishing?"

"Yeah. You know, it's when you, uh, try to separate the little fishies from the water they're swimming in. People have been doing it for a long time."

"This isn't funny," I snap. "This isn't some fuckin' joke."

"You're right. Most people taking fishing very seriously."

I turn to leave.

I've had it.

Had it with this night. With this morning.

I've had it with these goddamn lunatics.

I resolve to do what I should have done hours ago, which is to take care of myself first and get myself the fuck home.

"You saw me earlier tonight, didn't you?" Shane asks rhetorically. "On top of Mount Royal."

I stop.

I breathe.

I turn back around.

"What were you doing up there?"

"Taking my shift."

"Your shift?"

"We all take shifts," he says, casting his eyes toward the water. "And in return, we get to fish."

I try to process this information. Try to focus it through the lens of reason. But keep coming up short in my efforts. My brain can only interpret what I've just learned as, at worst, the mad rantings of a drunken musician, and, at best, some kind of silly parable.

"Well, there better be some magical fuckin' fish in that little pond then," I say, "if they're worth being crucified for."

"You're not too far off," Shane replies, smiling. "Only... there's just one fish."

"One fish?"

"Yep."

"So they,"—I point—"are all fishing for the same fish?"

"*Oui, monsieur*. You like salmon?"

"Meh," I reply.

"Well, I guess it's not about the flavor anyway. It's about what's *inside* the salmon that matters."

I can't help myself…

"Omega-3 fatty acids?"

Shane smiles, but it's a reluctant smile.

"Fine, tell me," I continue, indulging him, "What's in the salmon?"

"Knowledge."

"Knowledge?"

I'm now leaning harder than ever toward the "mad rantings" interpretation of Shane's story.

"I guess I'd rather just go to school for that," I say, "rather than, ya know, fish for it."

Shane's reluctant smile now morphs into a frown, and it's not just a surface-level, mouth-muscles-only frown—the wrinkles of his crow's feet have joined in.

"Are you even supposed to be here?" he asks, his tone darkening.

"I *definitely* don't think so," I reply, honestly, "But apparently Morrigan does."

"Morrigan," Shane echoes while scratching at the white peppering of stubble on his chin.

"Who is she?" I ask.

"You're about to find out."

♣

Walk to the base of the trunk, then go up.

Those were the instructions Shane had left me with before returning to his music.

Looking back over my shoulder, the little suspension bridge is now a mere silhouette. My friends, who are presumably still gathered around that little pool, have been rendered invisible.

When I finally reach the base of the trunk, when I'm close enough to caress its cracked, corrugated bark with my open palm, I repeat the second part of Shane's instructions:

"Then go up."

Scanning the trunk, I pray I'll discover an elevator, or an escalator, or, at the very least, a staircase.

What I end up finding is a ladder. And not even a *real* ladder, but some twisted, thorny affair, which seems to be a living extension of the tree—its meandering "rungs" consisting of a series of bumps and branches.

I grab the nearest handhold and begin hoisting myself upward.

This is one of those defining moments, I realize. This, right now, is the final stage of the hero's journey. The twelfth (or thirteenth?) labor. The moment everyone has been waiting for.

But the thing is… I'm just not that kind of guy.

So instead of climbing that deathtrap of a ladder, instead of allowing myself to be transformed into some kind of trope or archetype or cliché, I turn around.

And walk away.

Back the way I came.

Now, more determined than ever, to leave this place.

To wake up.

To be rid of this sick delusion.

I pick up my pace.

I run.

And just as I see the outline of the bridge come back into focus, I hear the rustling of feathers.

Large feathers.

A shadow dashes across the ground in front of me, coming and going in the blink of an eye.

A large shadow.

The whoosh of air, crackling with static electricity, washes over me a full second later, knocking me off my feet.

And just as quickly as it had begun, it ends.

Leathery talons wrap around my torso, delicate in their aim but powerful in their grasp.

As I levitate, all I can hear is the *flap-flap-flap* of the creature's massive wings, and all I can see is the black sheen of elegantly coiffed feathers.

♣

## Part IV: *Thump. Thump Thump.*

*Thump.*

*Thump thump.*

*Thump.*

*Thump thump.*

These are the sounds I awake to.

My joints ache. My head pounds. My tongue laps at an arid mouth. When I open my eyes, the brightness of the midday sun is overpowering. Dried leaves crackle beneath me as I try, and fail, to stand.

So many leaves.

Clinging to my clothes. Covering every inch of the ground. In some spots, the drifts reach several feet high, as if the leaves are working together to climb back into the very trees they've fallen from.

And there are *trees*—multiple, normal-sized ones. They surround the little clearing I've just woken up in.

I try to remember how I got here.

Try to figure out where *here* is.

Meanwhile, the thumping persists.

*Thump.*

*Thump thump.*

*Thump.*

*Thump thump.*

Then it dawns on me.

The trees.

The drums.

I'm somewhere on *mont Royal.*

Somewhere near the park.

The leaves next to me begin to rustle and now I am able to stand.

I jump to my feet, staggering away from the unseen threat. In the process, I trip over something else buried in the leaves.

Something else alive.

"Well, good morning, gorgeous," says that something else alive, which turns out to be Rory. "Looks like you had a fun night last night."

You can guess what type of smile he's smiling as he nods toward the spot where I had just been laying. There, emerging from the leaves, is a black-haired, red-lipped figure.

"Good morning, boys," says the clairvoyant woman.

"Good morning," Rory replies.

"I don't mean to be rude," the woman says, now on her feet, "but I've really got to be going. Last night didn't exactly turn out the way I had expected it to."

She glares in my direction.

I look down at the leaves.

"Thanks for letting us crash at your place," she continues, addressing Rory.

"Anytime," he says. "My grove is always open."

"I'll being seeing you around, Finn," is the last thing the clairvoyant woman says before walking off through the trees.

I have so many questions. So many theories. So many objectively insane thoughts devouring my brain's processing power.

"Rory—" I begin.

"No. Not now."

"When?"

"After breakfast."

And with that, Rory begins rummaging through the leaves, eventually producing a small red cooler, from which he removes bagels, cream cheese, and smoked salmon.

He doesn't have a knife, so we spread the cream cheese with our index fingers. Then we sit together and eat, listening to the sounds of drums and make-believe battle.

# THANKS FOR DROPPING BY

I hope your thirst for urban Celtic fantasy has been thoroughly quenched by the assortment of stories you discovered inside *Neon Druid.*

And while we—the authors of said stories—do not accept tips, we do ask that you **please consider leaving *Neon Druid* a review on Amazon and/or Goodreads** if you'd like to show your appreciation.

Your review will help more people uncover this anthology so they too can cross over into the Celtic Otherworld. May the light of the Five Stars guide their souls.

*Mise le meas,*
**I. E. Kneverday**
Editor, *Neon Druid*

# ABOUT THE AUTHORS

### Madison McSweeney

Madison McSweeney is a horror and fantasy writer who has been published in *Zombie Punks F*** Off*, *Deadman's Tome*, *Unnerving Magazine*, *Women in Horror Annual Vol. 2*, and others. She lives in Ottawa, Canada with her family and her cat.

### Patrick Winters

Patrick Winters is a graduate of Illinois College in Jacksonville, IL, where he earned a degree in English Literature and Creative Writing. He has been published in the likes of *Sanitarium Magazine*, *Deadman's Tome*, *Trysts of Fate*, and other such titles. A full list of his previous publications may be found at his author's site, if you are so inclined to know: http://wintersauthor.azurewebsites.net/Publications/List

### Alexandra Brandt

Alexandra Brandt's debut fantasy short story, "We, the Ocean," was featured on the Tangent Online 2017 Recommended Reading List. She has sold stories to the *Fiction River Anthology Magazine* and other short fiction publications. Her portal fantasy short-story series, Wyndside Stories, is based on her love of Edinburgh and has contributed fiction to several anthologies and her own collection of fairy short stories, *Magic for a Rainy Day*. She writes nonfiction copy and does graphic design work, including freelance book cover design. You can find her online (and get a free short story) at alexandrajbrandt.com.

### Jennifer Lee Rossman

Jennifer Lee Rossman is an autistic and disabled lover of all things weird and mythical. Her work has been featured in several anthologies, and she co-edited *Love & Bubbles*, a queer anthology of underwater romance. Her debut novel, *Jack Jetstark's Intergalactic Freakshow*, is now available from World Weaver Press. She tweets @JenLRossman and blogs at jenniferleerossman.blogspot.com.

## Matthew Stevens

Matthew Stevens spent years dreaming about being a writer before he found time late at night after the house was asleep to create characters and worlds and the stories for them to inhabit. During the daylight hours, he balances many jobs; husband, stay-at-home dad, server at a local brew pub, and all-encompassing geek. His current projects find him dabbling in a wide range of genres from his drafted novel, a paranormal thriller, to numerous fantasy and sci-fi shorts, along with an occasional blog post examining his perspective on his own writing journey and any intriguing geeky topic that catches his attention. He can be found online at:
Facebook: https://www.facebook.com/matthewstevensauthor
Twitter: @matt_the_writer
Blog: theedgeofeverything.wordpress.com

## Tom Howard

Tom Howard is a fantasy and science fiction short story writer living in Little Rock, Arkansas. He thanks his friends and family for their inspiration and the Central Arkansas Speculative Fiction Writers' Group for their perspiration.

## Hailey Piper

Hailey Piper was born obsessed with monsters, ghosts, and all things that go bump in the night. She now writes horror stories to feed that obsession. Her work may be found in *Trickster's Treats*, *Five on the Fifth*, and the horror anthology *Thuggish Itch: Devilish.*

## Serena Jayne

Serena Jayne received her MFA in Writing Popular Fiction from Seton Hill University, and is a member of Romance Writers of America and Sisters in Crime. She's worked as a research scientist, a fish stick slinger, a chat wrangler, and a race horse narc. When she isn't trolling art museums for works that move her, she enjoys writing in multiple fiction genres. While her first love is all things paranormal, the mundane world provides plenty of story ideas.

## R. J. Howell

R. J. Howell is a writer, an artist, and a library assistant. She holds a BA in Fiction Writing from Columbia College Chicago and is currently working toward her MFA in Popular Fiction at Stonecoast. Her short fiction has been published in *JayHenge Publishing's Unearthly Sleuths* and *Unrealpolitik* anthologies. She's a firm believer in living a life well-read.

## P. J. Richards

P. J. Richards lives in Somerset, England, surrounded by the landscape, history and folklore she loves. Her short stories have been published in several anthologies. When not writing or drawing she can be found living in castles, shooting her longbow. Twitter: @P_J_Richards

## Art Lasky

Art is a retired computer programmer. After forty years of writing in COBOL and Assembler he decided to try writing in English; it's much harder than it looks. He lives in New York City with his wife/muse and regularly visiting grandkids. Art's had stories published in *Drunken Boat*, *Third Flat Iron Anthologies*, *The Lane of Unusual Traders*, *Fall Into Fantasy*, *The Rabbit Hole*, *Crypt-Gnats* and *Home Planet News Online*. You can contact him at ALASKY9679@YAHOO.COM

## Ed Ahern

Ed Ahern resumed writing after forty odd years in foreign intelligence and international sales. He's had two over hundred stories and poems published so far, and three books. Ed works the other side of writing at Bewildering Stories, where he sits on the review board and manages a posse of five review editors.

## E.K. Reisinger

From chronicling an Alaskan cruise to researching the manuscripts of the Medieval Egyptian desert, writer E.K. Reisinger explores a love of culture and history in her twenty-year career as a journalist, writer and editor. She's also held managerial positions at Greenspring Media Group, Thomson Reuters and, most recently, the Hill Museum & Manuscript Library (HMML) at Saint John's University. HMML holds the world's largest collection of resources for the study of manuscript cultures. Now, Reisinger writes fantasy and romance from her office in rural Minnesota. Among other accolades, Reisinger is a former news reporting and writing fellow with The Poynter Institute in St. Petersburg, Florida. She is also a general member of the Romance Writers of America. See more about her at www.ekreisinger.com or on Twitter: @ekreisinger.

### Jarret Keene

Jarret Keene is an Assistant Professor in Residence in the English Department at the University of Nevada, Las Vegas, where he teaches creative writing and ancient and medieval literature. His fiction, essays, and verse have appeared in literary journals like *New England Review*, *Carolina Quarterly*, and the *Southeast Review*. He has written books—travel guide, unauthorized rock-band biography, poetry collections—and edited acclaimed and landmark short-fiction anthologies like *Las Vegas Noir* and *Dead Neon: Tales of Near-Future Las Vegas*. For more than a decade, Keene was the contributing music editor at *Vegas Seven* magazine and a book critic for *Tucson Weekly*. Before becoming a professor, he edited alt-weeklies and wrote casino-employee newsletters. Keene is currently writing a critical analysis of auteur works by comic-book legend Jack Kirby.

### Willow Croft

Willow Croft is a freelance writer and poet who currently lives in the high desert but dreams of a home by a tumultuous ocean. When not writing, she cares for her rescued stray calico and two very fat TNR feral cats.

### Laila Amado

Laila Amado is a migrating scientist, currently adapting to island life somewhere in the world. She writes fairy tales, dark fantasy, and, occasionally, science fiction. You can find her on Twitter @onbonbon7

## I. E. Kneverday

Hi, it's me again, I. E. Kneverday, editor of *Neon Druid* and mischief-maker-in-chief at Mt. Misery Press. A bit about myself: Grew up in Boston. Got schooled up in Montreal. Currently living in San Jose with my wife and two polydactyl cats. My short fiction has been featured in publications and anthologies including *Drabbledark*, *Enchanted Conversation Magazine*, *Chronos*, and *Exoplanet Magazine*. My first collection of short stories, *The Woburn Chronicles: A Trio of Supernatural Tales Set in New England's Most Mysterious City*, is available now. Learn more at Kneverday.com and come say hi on Twitter (@Kneverday).

# INDEX

*Celtic Gods, Goddesses, Heroes, & Monsters*

## *Cities, Towns, and Other Locations*

# ALSO FROM MT. MISERY PRESS

The Woburn Chronicles:
A Trio of Supernatural Tales Set in
New England's Most Mysterious City

*by I. E. Kneverday*

Shape-shifting leprechauns (1919). Mad scientist-sorcerers (1979). Haunted pine groves (2009). In Woburn, they've all been chronicled. A collection of three (interconnected) short stories, *The Woburn Chronicles* mixes historical fiction and urban fantasy, with a dash of Boston-Irish wit thrown in for good measure.

Available Now on Amazon

Made in the USA
Middletown, DE
11 January 2019